THE SCENT OF BREAD, BLOOD AND BELONGING

by Chris Koningen

Copyright © 2025 Christopher Koningen

All rights reserved

The characters and events portrayed in this book are fictitious. Any similarity to real persons, living or dead, is coincidental and not intended by the author.

No part of this book may be reproduced, or stored in a retrieval system, or transmitted in any form or by any means, electronic, mechanical, photocopying, recording, or otherwise, without express written permission of the publisher.

Cover design by: Christopher Koningen

*For Tom, my incredible husband and best friend,
who has stood by me through life's every challenge.
Your unwavering support means everything.
I love you.*

*For my wonderful family and friends,
thank you for listening, for understanding,
and for helping me feel a little less alone
on my dark days.*

*For all those who have been,
and continue to be, persecuted around the world
for the simple act of being themselves:
this story is for you, you are not alone.*

AUTHOR'S NOTE

World War II and the Holocaust have captivated my interest since childhood. Now at 39, I find myself still drawn to this pivotal moment in history—not just for its historical significance, but for the deeply human stories that continue to resonate today.

As I researched and read over the years, I noticed how certain narratives remain underrepresented in historical fiction. While the Jewish experience during the Holocaust has been documented in many powerful works—as it absolutely should be—the stories of other persecuted groups often receive less attention. The experiences of homosexuals, Roma and Sinti people, the physically and mentally disabled, political dissidents, prisoners of war, and others targeted simply for being different deserve to be remembered as well, filling in the parts of this tragic history that sometimes remain in shadow.

This book emerged from my desire to illuminate one such story—a young man in occupied Netherlands forced to hide both his Jewish heritage and his homosexuality. While the characters in this novel are entirely fictional, I was struck by the particular burden of someone concealing multiple identities, vulnerable not only to Nazi persecution but also to rejection from his own community. What must it have been like to live with such secrets, to navigate a world where either revelation could mean devastation?

I'm troubled by the parallels I see in our modern world. The distance between us and the events of the Holocaust grows with each passing year, and with it, I fear we're losing grasp of its essential warnings. The rhetoric of division, the scapegoating of minority groups, the casual dehumanisation of "others"—these dangerous currents feel increasingly familiar.

This isn't just a historical novel to me. It's my attempt to connect readers with those who lived under impossible circumstances, who simply wanted to exist freely as themselves without fear. Through this character's journey, I hope to remind us what happens when hatred is normalised and difference becomes dangerous.

I wrote this book from a place of genuine concern and care—for the memories of those who suffered, and for our shared responsibility to recognise similar patterns when they emerge today. If these pages help even one person see the humanity in those who are marginalised or different, then this work has served its purpose.

In a world quick to draw lines between "us" and "them," I hope this story serves as a gentle reminder that we are, in our hopes and vulnerabilities, far more alike than different.

CHAPTER 1: THE BAKER'S BOY

Rotterdam, 1917-1932

I was born in Rotterdam in the autumn of 1917, beneath a sky that smelled of coal smoke and salt from the Maas River. My mother said I came into the world screaming, a tiny thing with a head of thick black hair and a face too angular for a baby. My father, a quiet man, simply nodded when he saw me. "A strong face," he said. "He'll grow into it."

But I never really did. By the time I was fifteen, I was still short for a Dutchman, still thin, with sharp cheekbones that made people glance twice. "Handsome, in a peculiar way," I once overheard a woman say. It wasn't meant as a compliment.

Our family lived in a modest apartment in the Jewish quarter, just a few tram stops from the heart of the city. The building was narrow and tall, like most in Rotterdam, with steep stairs that my mother complained about whenever she carried groceries up to our third-floor home. The wallpaper in our front room was faded blue, peeling slightly at the corners where damp crept in during winter. But my mother kept it clean, almost obsessively so. "A home should smell of soap, not poverty," she would say.

My father was a tailor who specialised in men's suits. His shop was on the ground floor of a building two streets away, where he spent his days hunched over fine fabrics, his fingers perpetually stained with blue chalk marks. He was a man of few words, but his hands spoke volumes—precise, gentle, creating order from chaos with each stitch. At night, he would return home smelling of wool and tobacco, his shoulders stooped from bending over his work all day.

I had two older brothers, both broad-shouldered and blond like my mother's side of the family. Pieter was five years older than me, already apprenticed to my father by the time I was ten. He had our father's steady hands and quiet determination. Jan was three years my senior, loud and confident, with an easy charm that drew people to him. He was always surrounded by friends, always at the centre of some adventure.

I was the odd one out in every way.

"Are you sure he's yours, Jacob?" I once heard a neighbour joke to my father as they stood smoking outside our building. My father hadn't responded, but the question lingered in my mind like a splinter.

At school, the differences became more pronounced. While my brothers excelled at sports and made friends easily, I preferred the library's quiet corners. I devoured books, losing myself in stories of far-off places and different lives. My teachers praised my essays but worried about my reluctance to join in games with the other boys.

"He's too serious," they told my mother at meetings. "He needs to play more."

But play felt foreign to me, a language I couldn't quite grasp. When forced to join football matches in the dusty schoolyard, I would hover at the edges, praying the ball wouldn't come my way. The other boys noticed, of course. Children always sense weakness.

"Arthijs is afraid of the ball!" they would taunt. "Are you a girl, Arthijs?"

I wasn't afraid of the ball. I was afraid of the attention, of standing out even more than I already did.

Home wasn't much better. Our apartment was small, and privacy was a luxury none of us could afford. My brothers shared a room, their beds pushed against opposite walls, the space between them cluttered with their shared lives—boots kicked off after a day's work, a collection of smooth stones Jan had gathered from the riverbank, Pieter's carefully folded clothes.

I slept on a narrow bed in what had once been a storage closet, barely wide enough for me to stretch out my arms. But I loved that tiny room. It was mine alone, a sanctuary where I could read without Jan teasing me or Pieter sighing impatiently at the lamp burning late into the night.

On Fridays, our home transformed. My mother would spend the day cooking for Shabbat, the apartment filling with the scents of chicken soup simmering and fresh challah baking. The table would be covered with a white cloth, the silver candlesticks polished until they gleamed. As dusk fell, she would light the candles, her hands moving in gentle circles as she welcomed the Sabbath.

My father would recite the Kiddush over wine, his voice deeper and more melodic than his everyday speech. It was the only time I ever heard him sing. Those moments—the soft glow of candles, the taste of sweet wine on my lips, the familiar rhythm of prayers—were when I felt most connected to my family, to our history.

But even then, I was aware of a distance between us, as if I were watching them through a rain-streaked window.

When I was twelve, I found a book of poetry in the back of our local library, hidden behind heavier volumes on a bottom shelf. The pages were worn soft with use, the spine cracked from being opened too many times at the same passages. I don't remember the poet's name now, but I remember how his words made me feel seen, for the first time. Understood.

I copied one poem into a small notebook I kept hidden beneath my mattress. At night, I would read it by the thin beam of moonlight that slipped through my window, whispering the words like a prayer:

The heart has chambers like a house
With doors we dare not open
For fear of what might dwell within
Or worse, what might escape

I didn't fully understand what those words meant then, but they resonated in me like a struck bell.

Rotterdam itself was a city of contrasts, much like my family. The old and new stood side by side—medieval churches next to modern office buildings, horse-drawn carts sharing streets with automobiles. The heart of the city was constantly evolving, reaching toward the future, while the outskirts moved at a slower pace, clinging to tradition.

Our neighbourhood was one of these slower places. The Jewish quarter wasn't marked on any official map, but everyone knew its boundaries. The streets were narrower here, the buildings closer together. The air smelled of different spices, different cooking. On Saturdays, a hush would fall as families observed Shabbat, though my father's shop remained open—a compromise between faith and necessity that I could see pained him.

Beyond our neighbourhood lay the rest of Rotterdam, a world I explored whenever I could escape my chores. I loved the harbour most of all. The Maas River was the city's lifeblood, carrying ships from all over the world to our docks. I would sit for hours watching the vessels come and go, imagining the distant places they had been.

The smell of the harbour was intoxicating—salt water and tar, fish and spices, the sweet rot of timber and the metallic tang of industry. It was the smell of possibility, of elsewhere. Sometimes I would close my eyes and breathe deeply, pretending I was on one of those ships, heading out to sea, to a place where no one knew me or expected anything from me.

When I was fourteen, I found work delivering messages for businesses along the harbour. The pay was meagre, but it gave me an excuse to wander the city, to observe its rhythms and secrets. I learned which alleys provided shortcuts between major streets, which cafes would give a hungry boy leftover bread at the end of the day, which policemen would look the other way if you ran a little too fast down a crowded sidewalk.

It was during these deliveries that I first began to notice other differences in myself—differences that had nothing to do with my appearance or my interests.

It started with a dockworker, a man with shoulders like boulders and hands rough as tree bark. He was unloading crates from a ship, his shirt sticking to his back with sweat, muscles rippling beneath tanned skin. I found myself staring, my message forgotten in my hand, a strange tightness in my chest. When he caught me looking, I fled, my face burning with a shame I didn't understand.

Similar moments followed. A young shopkeeper with kind eyes and a gentle laugh. A student reading poetry by the canal, his fingers long and elegant as they turned the pages. Each time, the same inexplicable pull, the same confusion afterward, the same burning shame.

I told no one, of course. I barely had words for what I was feeling. But I knew it was wrong—or at least, that others would think it was. I had heard the slurs boys at school used, seen the disgust on men's faces when they spoke of "those types." I knew enough to be afraid.

So, I buried these feelings deep, adding another layer to the differences that already separated me from everyone else. I focused instead on school, on work, on surviving each day without drawing too much attention to myself.

When I was fifteen, I saw two men in a shadowed doorway near the harbour. They stood too close together, their hands touching in a way that couldn't be mistaken for friendship. I froze, unable to look away. Something inside me recognised itself in them—a reflection in a mirror I hadn't known existed.

One of the men saw me watching. Our eyes met for a single, terrifying moment. Then he pulled away from his companion, his face hardening into a mask. "What are you looking at, boy?" he snapped. "Get lost!"

I ran, my heart hammering against my ribs, not stopping until I reached the familiar streets of our neighbourhood. That night, I tore my poem from its hiding place and burned it in the small coal stove that heated our apartment, watching the words curl and blacken in the flames.

By the time I turned fifteen, Rotterdam was changing. The Great War had ended, but its effects lingered. Money was tight, and tensions ran beneath the surface of daily life like an electric current. New buildings rose across the city, taller and more modern than before. Automobiles replaced more horse-drawn carts each year. Radio sets appeared in cafes and wealthy homes, bringing news and music from across Europe.

My brothers embraced these changes. Jan saved for months to buy a second-hand radio, which he tinkered with endlessly, pulling in stations from as far away as Paris and London. Pieter talked of electric sewing machines that would revolutionise my father's business. They looked forward, eager for the future.

I found myself looking backward, clinging to the Rotterdam I knew. I memorised the city as it was, storing away sensory details as if preparing for a time when they would be gone: the creak of the wooden drawbridge near our home as it rose to let ships pass; the call of the herring seller who wheeled his cart through our street every Wednesday; the pattern of sunlight through the stained glass windows of the old church we passed on the way to school; the sweet-sour smell of the brewery two blocks from my father's shop.

One day, as I helped my father in his shop, measuring fabric for a customer, I caught him watching me with an odd expression.

"What?" I asked, suddenly self-conscious.

He studied me for a moment longer, then said quietly, "You see things others don't, Arthijs."

It wasn't a question, and I didn't know how to respond. My father rarely spoke directly to me, and never about anything beyond work or school or family obligations.

"Is that bad?" I finally asked.

He considered this, his hands continuing to work the fabric even as his eyes remained on me. "No," he said after a long pause. "But it can be lonely."

We never spoke of it again. But something shifted between us that day—a small acknowledgment of my difference that felt, for once, not like a failing but simply a fact.

In 1932, the year I turned fifteen, Rotterdam experienced one of the coldest winters in memory. The canals froze solid, and for weeks the city transformed into a wonderland of ice. People skated to work, goods were transported on sleds, and impromptu markets sprang up on the frozen waterways.

I remember standing on the Maas with my brothers, the three of us balanced on borrowed skates. For once, we were equals—all of us equally clumsy, equally laughing, equally alive in the sharp, clean cold. The sky above was a clear, painful blue, and around us, the city sparkled like something out of a fairy tale.

It was one perfect day in a childhood of feeling apart. I held onto it like a talisman in the years that followed, a reminder that even in a world where I never quite fit, there were moments of belonging. Moments when the differences that defined me didn't matter.

I couldn't have known then how much I would need that memory. Couldn't have imagined how soon the Rotterdam I knew would vanish like breath in winter air. Couldn't have guessed that standing on that frozen river was the last time I would feel truly part of my family, my city, my world.

But perhaps some part of me sensed it. Perhaps that's why, as Jan and Pieter raced ahead, I paused to look back at the city skyline—the church spires and modern towers, the peaked roofs and smoking chimneys, all etched sharp against that perfect sky. Committing it to memory. Saying goodbye before I knew I needed to.

CHAPTER 2: THE APPRENTICE

Rotterdam, 1933-1935

No one in my family was surprised when I chose not to follow my father and Pieter into tailoring. My hands, unlike theirs, were impatient with the precision of stitches, the delicate negotiation with fabric and thread. What did surprise them was my alternative.

"A baker?" my mother repeated, her brow furrowed as we sat around our dinner table in the spring of 1933. "But why, Arthijs?"

I struggled to explain something I barely understood myself. How could I tell her about the peace I felt when I watched the baker on our street transform simple ingredients into something nourishing? How the scent of fresh bread made me feel safe in a way little else did? How, unlike tailoring—where every stitch was visible, every mistake apparent—baking seemed to allow for a different kind of precision, one hidden within the mysterious chemistry of flour and water and heat?

"It's honest work," my father said finally, breaking the uncomfortable silence. "Meneer de Vries is a good man. Jewish. Respected." He nodded once, decisively. "He will teach you well."

And so, just after my sixteenth birthday, I became an apprentice at de Vries Bakery on Hoogstraat, near the old harbour. The shop was small but well-established, with a reputation for quality that drew customers from across Rotterdam. The bakery itself was in the back, a cavernous room dominated by two large brick ovens, their iron doors blackened from years of fire.

On my first day, Meneer de Vries handed me a heavy canvas apron, stained with the ghosts of past loaves. "You'll earn a clean one," he said, his voice as rough as pumpernickel. "When you prove you're serious."

My mentor was a man of contradictions. His hands were massive, with thick fingers that seemed too clumsy for the delicate work they performed, yet I never saw him break so much as an egg yolk. His face was stern, creased with lines that deepened when he concentrated, but his eyes—a warm amber, like honey held up to light—could crinkle with unexpected kindness. He was a master of his craft, exacting and sometimes merciless in his standards, yet I never once heard him raise his voice.

Those first weeks were a baptism by fire and flour. I arrived at four each morning, my eyes gritty with sleep, to find Meneer de Vries already at work, his broad back bent over the mixing trough. My tasks were menial—stoking the ovens, hauling sacks of flour, scrubbing surfaces until my hands were raw—but I watched everything.

I watched how he mixed the dough, his massive hands gentle as they coaxed flour and water into cohesion. I watched how he sensed the precise moment bread was done, not by time but by the smell, the colour, the hollow sound when he tapped the bottom of a loaf. I watched, and I learned, and slowly, I began to understand the language of bread.

The bakery was a symphony of sensations. The soft give of dough beneath my palms. The yeasty tang in the air as fermentation worked its slow magic. The crack and whisper of a fresh loaf cooling on the rack. The golden warmth of the ovens that turned winter mornings bearable and summer days nearly unbearable. These textures and smells and sounds became more familiar to me than the inside of my family's apartment.

"Bread is alive," Meneer de Vries told me one morning, three months into my apprenticeship. He had finally allowed me to mix a batch of simple white dough, and I was nervous, my movements stiff. "Not just the yeast. The whole thing. It breathes. It responds to your touch, to the weather, to your mood." He placed his hand on my shoulder. "Relax. Listen to what it tells you."

I tried to do as he said, to feel the life in the mixture beneath my hands. At first, it was just sticky resistance, but then—as the gluten developed and the dough began to come together—I felt what he meant. A subtle transformation, a gathering cohesion. The separate ingredients becoming something new, something unified.

"There," he said, nodding with approval. "Now you're beginning to understand."

Meneer de Vries was not an effusive man, and his praise was rare enough that this simple affirmation left me glowing for days.

The work was physically demanding. My arms ached from kneading, my back from bending over the workbench, my legs from standing for twelve, sometimes fourteen hours a day. I fell into bed each night exhausted, my dreams filled with the rhythmic motion of shaping loaves. But for the first time in my life, I felt purposeful. The ache in my muscles was a badge of accomplishment, the flour embedded in the creases of my hands a mark of belonging.

My family noticed the change in me. "You stand straighter," my mother remarked one Sunday when I visited. She reached up to brush flour from my collar, a habitual gesture even though I had bathed and changed before coming home. "And you smile more."

I hadn't realised it myself, but she was right. The bakery had given me something my family, for all their love, never could: a place where my differences didn't matter. Where what counted was not whether I fit some predetermined mould, but whether I could learn, adapt, create.

By the winter of 1933, Meneer de Vries had begun to trust me with more complex tasks. I learned to make the rich, egg-glazed challah we sold on Fridays, the delicate pastries filled with almond paste, the dense rye bread favoured by the dockworkers. Each success was a small triumph; each failure—and there were many—a lesson I absorbed hungrily.

One frigid February morning, I arrived to find Meneer de Vries hunched over the workbench, his face drawn with pain. He straightened as I entered, but I had seen the grimace he couldn't quite hide.

"Your back again?" I asked, hanging my coat on the hook by the door.

He grunted, neither confirming nor denying, but the way he moved—carefully, as if his spine might shatter with any sudden gesture—told me all I needed to know. His back had been troubling him for weeks, though he refused to see a doctor or take a day off.

"I'll handle the heavy lifting today," I said, rolling up my sleeves. It wasn't the first time I had made this offer, but it was the first time he didn't immediately dismiss it.

"We'll see," was all he said, but I knew I had won a small victory.

By midday, it was clear he could barely stand. When the lunch rush ended and the shop was momentarily empty, I steered him firmly to a chair. "Rest," I insisted. "I can manage the afternoon alone."

He started to protest, then winced as his back spasmed. "Fine," he conceded grudgingly. "But only for an hour."

That hour stretched into the rest of the day. I worked frantically, determined to prove I could handle the responsibility. When the last customer left and I finally had time to check on him, I found him asleep in the chair, his breathing deep and even. I covered him with a blanket and finished cleaning up as quietly as I could.

The next morning, he arrived at the usual time, moving stiffly but with determination. As we worked side by side, preparing the day's first batches, he said without looking at me, "You did well yesterday. The customers noticed no difference."

From Meneer de Vries, this was high praise indeed.

"Thank you," I said, trying to hide my pleasure.

He was silent for a moment, his hands working a mound of dough with practiced efficiency. Then he cleared his throat. "I've been thinking. The room upstairs—the small one at the back. It's just storage now, but it could be made liveable." He glanced at me. "If you wanted to move in."

I stared at him, my hands stilling in the dough. "Move in?"

He shrugged, a gesture that clearly cost him some pain. "You're here all hours anyway. Might save you the commute. And..." He hesitated. "It would be good to have someone in the building. In case my back goes out again."

It was a practical suggestion, presented in practical terms. But I understood the offer behind it—not just a room, but trust. Independence. A place that was mine in a way my closet-sized bedroom at home could never be.

"I would like that," I said, trying to match his matter-of-fact tone despite the excitement bubbling in my chest. "Thank you."

He nodded once; the matter settled. "We'll clean it out this weekend."

The room was indeed small, little bigger than my space at home, with a slanted ceiling that meant I could stand upright only in the centre. But it had a window that overlooked the quiet back street, a washbasin in the corner, and enough space for a narrow bed and a small table with a chair. Meneer de Vries had the floor repaired where it sagged, installed a new lock on the door, and even found a faded but clean rug to cover the bare boards.

"It's nothing fancy," he said gruffly as we surveyed the finished space. "But it'll keep the rain off your head."

"It's perfect," I told him, and meant it.

Moving my belongings took less than an hour. I had few possessions—some clothes, a handful of books, a photograph of my family taken when I was twelve. My mother wept a little when I told her I was leaving, but I think she understood that this was a step I needed to take. My father simply clasped my shoulder and told me to visit on Sundays. My brothers were too busy with their own lives to care much either way.

Those first nights alone were strange. The building creaked and settled in ways different from our apartment. The smells were different—yeast and flour rather than my mother's cooking and my father's pipe tobacco. The sounds were different—the distant rumble of the early morning delivery carts rather than my brothers' snoring through the thin wall.

But I quickly grew to love the solitude. For the first time in my life, I had privacy, true privacy. No one to question why I read late into the night, or why I sometimes stared out the window for hours, watching the street below. No one to notice which pages in my books were most worn from rereading, or to ask about the poems I had begun to write in a small notebook—tentative verses that tried to capture the beauty I found in ordinary things: the perfect curve of a risen loaf, the play of light through my window at dawn, the strength in Meneer de Vries's flour-dusted hands.

Living above the bakery also meant I became more deeply embedded in the rhythm of the business. I was often the first one down in the morning now, lighting the ovens and starting the day's first dough. Customers began to know me by name, to ask for me specifically when they had special requests. I wasn't just an apprentice anymore; I was becoming a baker in my own right.

One evening in the late summer of 1934, as we cleaned up after closing, Meneer de Vries mentioned casually that he was thinking of hiring another assistant.

"Business is good," he said, wiping down the marble countertop. "We could use another pair of hands."

I felt an unexpected twinge of jealousy at the thought of sharing my place, my mentor. But I merely nodded. "Anyone in mind?"

He hesitated, his cloth pausing on the counter. "There's a young man, a refugee from Germany. Jewish. His family fled Berlin last year." He resumed cleaning, his movements more deliberate. "He worked in a bakery there. Knows his trade. But no one will hire him."

"Because he's German?" I asked.

Meneer de Vries's mouth tightened. "Because he's Jewish and German. Neither is very popular these days."

It was the first time he had directly referenced the changing political climate. We heard things, of course—news from Germany about the new chancellor, Hitler, and his policies against Jews. Rumours of businesses seized, of people disappearing. But it had seemed distant, a foreign problem that wouldn't touch us here in Rotterdam.

"What's happening over there," I began cautiously, "could it happen here?"

Meneer de Vries was silent for a long moment. Then he sighed, a deep, weary sound. "I don't know, Arthijs. I hope not. The Netherlands has always been tolerant. But..." He gestured vaguely eastward. "There are those who admire what Hitler is doing. Who think he has the right ideas."

I thought of the graffiti I had seen recently on a wall near the harbour—crude antisemitic slogans I had tried to ignore. Of the whispers among customers when Jewish merchants were mentioned. Of the new political pamphlets being handed out in the market square.

"The world is changing," Meneer de Vries continued, his voice low. "Not for the better, I think. But we go on. We work. We live." He looked at me directly, his amber eyes serious. "And we help others when we can. So, this young man—David is his name. David Cohen. I'll bring him in tomorrow. You'll show him how we do things here."

I nodded, understanding that this was more than just a business decision. It was a small stand against the tide rising around us. "I'll teach him everything you've taught me."

Meneer de Vries smiled, a rare full smile that transformed his stern face. "I know you will." Then he clapped me on the shoulder. "Now go get some sleep. Tomorrow will be busy."

I climbed the stairs to my room that night with a strange mixture of feelings—pride that Meneer de Vries trusted me to train someone else, curiosity about this David Cohen, and a nagging unease about the changes Meneer de Vries had spoken of.

From my window, I could see a slice of Rotterdam's skyline, the familiar towers and spires silhouetted against the night sky. The city looked as it always had, solid and eternal. I told myself that whatever was happening in Germany couldn't touch us here. That Rotterdam—practical, tolerant Rotterdam—would remain unchanged.

I didn't yet understand how quickly the world could transform, how easily the familiar could become strange, how swiftly safety could turn to danger. I was seventeen, with my own room and a trade I loved. The future stretched before me, seemingly solid as bread.

And tomorrow, I would meet David Cohen, never suspecting how that meeting would change everything.

CHAPTER 3: SECRETS

Rotterdam, 1936-1938

David Cohen changed everything.

Not all at once—that isn't how life works—but gradually, like yeast working through dough, invisible until suddenly the whole mass has transformed. By 1936, he had been at the bakery for nearly two years, and we had fallen into a comfortable rhythm. We worked well together, anticipating each other's movements in the small space behind the counter, passing tools without needing to speak. His German accent had softened, though it still emerged when he was tired or excited, rolling his words into unfamiliar shapes that I found oddly endearing.

David was everything I wasn't. Where I was quiet, he was quick to laugh. Where I observed, he participated. He charmed the elderly women who came for their daily bread, teased the children who pressed their noses against our display window, engaged the dock workers in animated conversations about politics and football. When he entered a room, it brightened, as if someone had opened a curtain to let in more light.

And I noticed. God help me, I noticed everything about him.

I noticed how the morning sun caught in his dark curls, turning them almost auburn. I noticed the small scar on his left thumb, legacy of a childhood accident with a bread knife. I noticed how he hummed under his breath while kneading dough, mostly Bach, though sometimes folk songs from his German childhood. I noticed the exact shade of his eyes—

amber like Meneer de Vries's, but flecked with green near the pupil. I noticed, and I tried desperately not to notice that I was noticing.

We shared the attic now, Meneer de Vries having partitioned the space into two small rooms shortly after David arrived. A thin wall separated us, and at night, I would lie awake listening to the soft sounds of his breathing, the creak of his bed when he turned, occasionally a murmured word in German as he dreamed.

Torture and comfort, all at once.

I had long ago accepted what I was—not accepted, perhaps, but acknowledged. The knowledge sat in me like a stone, heavy and immovable. I had grown accustomed to the weight of it, had learned to navigate life around its presence. It was a private truth, something no one needed to know. Something that couldn't hurt me as long as I never gave it voice.

But David made silence harder. His presence awakened something in me that I had managed to keep dormant through sheer force of will. The careful barriers I had constructed began to crack, letting dangerous light spill through.

One evening in March 1936, we were closing up the shop together. Meneer de Vries had gone home early with a head cold, trusting us to finish the day's work. A late winter storm had blown in from the sea, and the streets were nearly empty, most people having hurried home ahead of the icy rain.

David was wiping down the marble counter, humming softly. The warm light from the lamps caught in his hair, on his skin, making him glow against the darkening shop. I was supposed to be sweeping, but my broom had stilled, and I was simply watching him, unable to look away.

He glanced up and caught me staring. Something shifted in his expression—a question, perhaps, or a recognition. The moment stretched between us, fragile as spun sugar.

Then he smiled, a different smile than his usual easy grin. This was smaller, more private. More real.

"What?" he asked softly.

I shook my head, unable to speak. Unable to lie. Unable to tell the truth.

David set down his cloth and crossed the small space between us. My heart hammered against my ribs, a terrified rhythm. He stopped just before me, close enough that I could smell the cinnamon and sugar that clung to his skin.

"Arthijs," he said, my name in his mouth sounding different, special. "I see you too."

Four simple words that cracked the world open.

I don't remember who moved first. Only that suddenly his hands were on my face, and mine were clutching the front of his shirt, and we were kissing as if the storm outside had somehow gotten into our blood, wild and inevitable.

When we broke apart, I was trembling. Not with fear—though fear would come later—but with the sheer overwhelming relief of finally, finally being known.

David's eyes searched mine, serious for once. "I've wanted to do that since the first day I arrived."

I swallowed hard. "Why didn't you?"

"I wasn't sure." His thumb brushed my cheek, a touch so gentle it nearly undid me. "Until now."

That night, in the narrow privacy of my room, with the storm lashing the windows and the thin wall between us suddenly an unbearable barrier, I made a decision I had never thought I would make. I opened my door and crossed the small landing to his.

I had thought, somehow, that this first step would be the hardest—this deliberate crossing of a threshold I had never permitted myself to approach. But when David opened his door, his hair tousled from sleep or its absence, his eyes wide with surprise and then something deeper, something hungry, I realised that the real courage would come later. The real test would be living with this secret in a world determined to punish it.

But that was a problem for tomorrow. Tonight belonged to us alone.

Dawn found us tangled together in his narrow bed, the storm having blown itself out to leave a pristine sky, clear and cold. I traced the line of his jaw with my finger, memorizing the feel of him, already dreading the moment we would have to become just colleagues again.

"What are you thinking?" David murmured, his voice rough with sleep.

"That we have to be careful," I replied.

He nodded, serious for once. "I know." Then a flash of his usual smile. "But not right now."

He drew me back to him, and for a little longer, the world outside ceased to exist.

Being with David taught me something I had never understood before: that happiness and fear could coexist in the same moment. That joy could be shot through with terror, like veins of darkness in marble. That love—and it was love, though we rarely spoke the word aloud—could be both salvation and danger.

We became experts at secrecy. In public, we maintained a careful distance, our interaction friendly but never too familiar. We developed a language of small gestures, coded remarks, glances that communicated volumes while remaining invisible to others. A brushed hand while passing the flour. A private smile across the bakery. Notes left in bread dough for the other to find while shaping loaves.

Only when we were truly alone—in our rooms late at night, or during rare shared days off spent in secluded spots along the Maas—could we be ourselves completely. Those moments were precious, hoarded like jewels, sustaining us through the constant vigilance that filled the rest of our days.

Meneer de Vries never spoke of what he must have suspected. But sometimes I would catch him watching us with a thoughtful expression, neither approving nor condemning. Occasionally, he would find reasons to send one of us on an errand, then casually mention that the other should go too, for company or assistance. Small kindnesses that we recognised but never acknowledged.

Our world narrowed to the bakery, our rooms, and the few safe havens we discovered in the city. But rather than feeling confined by this smaller existence, I found it richer, more vibrant than any life I had known before. David filled spaces in me I hadn't recognised were empty. He brought colour where there had been only grey.

And yet, as 1936 turned to 1937, shadows lengthened across Europe. News from Germany grew increasingly disturbing. More refugees arrived in Rotterdam each month, carrying stories that made the blood run cold. David's family received fewer and fewer letters from relatives who had remained behind, until communication stopped entirely with some of them.

David worried constantly about his younger sister and elderly grandparents still in Berlin. "I should go back," he would say during our darkest nights. "I should bring them out."

I would hold him tighter, selfishly grateful that his parents had forbidden such a journey. "They wouldn't let you back into the Netherlands," I would remind him. "You'd be trapped there too."

He knew I was right, but the knowledge didn't ease his guilt. I would feel him sometimes, awake in the early hours, his body tense with unspoken fears. All I could do was be there, offering what comfort my presence could provide.

The bakery became a gathering place for Rotterdam's growing community of German Jewish refugees. Meneer de Vries extended credit to those who couldn't pay, sometimes slipping extra loaves into bags when no one was looking.

David would speak with them in rapid German, collecting what news he could of conditions across the border, of who had escaped and who had disappeared.

I couldn't follow these conversations, but I saw their effect on him—how each report from his homeland carved new lines around his eyes, how his natural exuberance dimmed a little more with each passing month. I learned to read his moods in the way he kneaded dough—gently on good days, with barely restrained violence on bad ones.

"How do you stay so calm?" he asked me once, after a particularly grim account from a newly arrived family. "How do you not scream at what's happening?"

I had no good answer. I had always kept my emotions contained, had always observed rather than acted. It was my nature, just as it was his nature to feel everything with an intensity that sometimes frightened me.

"Someone has to keep baking the bread," I said finally, a feeble response that nevertheless made him smile.

"Always practical, my Arthijs," he murmured, resting his forehead against mine for a brief, stolen moment before we returned to work.

The bakery itself remained a haven, a small pocket of normality in an increasingly uncertain world. Regular customers continued their daily routines—Mevrouw Visser arriving precisely at eight each morning for her rye bread, Meneer Jansen purchasing the same two pastries every Sunday after church, the dock workers queuing for hot rolls during their mid-morning break.

These ordinary interactions anchored us, reminded us that despite everything, life continued. People still needed to eat. They still gathered to share news and gossip. They still celebrated birthdays and weddings with our cakes, still marked Shabbat with our challah, still found small comforts in the familiar scent of fresh bread.

I came to know our customers in ways I never had before. It was David who taught me this—how to see people not just as faces across a counter but as lives intersecting briefly with ours. He drew out their stories with his easy charm, remembered details about their families, their troubles, their small triumphs.

Reluctantly at first, then with growing interest, I began to absorb these stories. The elderly widow who bought a single roll each day, stretching her pension as far as possible. The harried mother of six whose rare smile when offered a free cookie for her youngest child became a private mission for David and me. The quiet man who came every Thursday for a loaf of dark bread and who, we eventually learned, had lost his wife in childbirth just months before.

Their lives flowed through our bakery like the river flowed through Rotterdam—constant, varied, carrying both joy and sorrow in its current. And like the river, they brought news from beyond our small world, whispers of changes that would eventually reach us all.

By 1938, those whispers had become shouts. In March, Germany annexed Austria. In November came Kristallnacht—the Night of Broken Glass—when Nazi storm troopers destroyed Jewish businesses and synagogues across Germany. The refugees arriving in Rotterdam now were shell-shocked, many having fled with nothing but the clothes they wore.

The bakery became more than just a place to buy bread. Meneer de Vries allowed community notices to be posted by the door, helping newcomers find housing and work. David organised an informal network to distribute food to those who couldn't afford it. I found myself teaching basic Dutch phrases to dazed German children while their parents spoke in hushed voices with David or Meneer de Vries.

Amidst this growing chaos, our private world became both more precious and more precarious. David and I clung to each other with increasing desperation, aware that what we had built could be swept away at any moment. Not just because of who we were to each other, but because of who we were in a world rapidly dividing into "us" and "them."

"Do you ever think of leaving?" David asked one night as we lay in my narrow bed, the sounds of the city muffled by the late hour. "Going somewhere far away from all of this?"

I considered the question, trying to imagine a life beyond Rotterdam, beyond the bakery. It was almost impossible. "Where would we go?"

"America, perhaps. Or England." He propped himself up on one elbow, his face serious in the dim light. "Somewhere they don't care that we're Jewish. Somewhere they might not care that we're..." He gestured between us, not finishing the sentence.

I reached up to trace the line of his brow, smoothing away the worry I found there. "Do such places exist?"

He caught my hand, pressing a kiss to the palm. "They must. The world is too big for everyone to hate us."

I wanted to believe him. But even then, in the spring of 1938, with war still a distant threat and the worst horrors still unimaginable, I sensed that there was nowhere far enough to run from what was coming. That the hatred spreading across Europe would not be easily escaped.

Instead of saying this, I pulled him closer. "We're safe here," I murmured, the lie tasting bitter on my tongue. "Rotterdam is different. The Netherlands is neutral. Nothing will happen to us."

He didn't argue, but I felt the tension in his body, the fear he couldn't quite suppress. We had both become practiced at these necessary deceptions, these comforting falsehoods we offered each other in the dark.

The truth was that Rotterdam was changing too. Small things at first—antisemitic graffiti appearing more frequently, the occasional hostile comment from a customer, Dutch friends becoming slightly more distant. Then larger shifts—fewer German Jewish refugees being granted residency permits, increased police presence in the Jewish quarter, heated political arguments breaking out even in our bakery.

One morning in late 1938, I arrived downstairs to find the shop window smeared with mud, a crude Star of David scratched into the grime. I cleaned it before Meneer de Vries or David could see, scrubbing until my hands were raw in the cold water. But I couldn't unsee it, couldn't unfeel the chill that had nothing to do with the winter air.

That evening, as the three of us sat in Meneer de Vries's small office reviewing the day's accounts, he cleared his throat uncharacteristically.

"I've been thinking," he said, his amber eyes moving between David and me. "About the future. About what might be prudent."

David tensed beside me. "What do you mean?"

Meneer de Vries sighed, suddenly looking much older than his fifty-odd years. "The world is changing, boys. Not for the better." He tapped his fingers against the accounts book. "I've been speaking with my cousin in America. In New York. He owns a bakery there too."

My heart began to pound. I knew what was coming before he said it.

"He could use good bakers. Both of you." Meneer de Vries looked directly at us. "He would sponsor you. Help with the paperwork."

David's hand found mine under the table, gripping tightly. "Both of us?" he asked, his voice carefully neutral.

Meneer de Vries nodded, his gaze steady. "Both of you. Together."

The words hung in the air, heavy with meaning. He knew. Of course he knew. And he was offering us a chance not just at safety, but at a life together away from the gathering storm.

"What about you?" I asked, my voice barely audible.

He smiled, a small, sad smile. "Rotterdam is my home. I was born here. I'll die here." His tone brooked no argument. "But you two are young. You should go while you still can."

Later that night, David and I argued in whispers, our words urgent, desperate. He wanted to go—not just for ourselves, but for his family. If he could establish himself in America, perhaps he could bring them over too. I wanted to stay—Rotterdam was the only home I had ever known, and the thought of leaving Meneer de Vries, my family, everything familiar, terrified me more than the uncertain future.

"We could be free there," David insisted, his eyes bright in the darkness. "Really free, Arthijs. To be together openly."

"You don't know that," I countered. "The whole world isn't as simple as you think."

"And it isn't as dark as you fear," he shot back. Then, more gently, "We have to try. What future do we have here, with things as they are?"

I had no answer for that. The truth was that I could imagine no future at all beyond the next day, the next week. The world had become too unpredictable, too threatening to permit long-term dreams.

In the end, we reached no decision that night. Or the next. The possibility of America hung between us, alternately alluring and terrifying, a potential escape hatch from a house that might soon be burning.

Throughout 1938, as conditions worsened across Europe, we continued our daily routine at the bakery. We rose before dawn, shaped the day's bread, served our customers, cleaned up, and began preparations for the next day. The familiar rhythm was a comfort, a scaffold supporting us through increasingly troubled times.

And in stolen moments—a brush of hands, a private smile, whispered conversations in the dark—we continued to build our secret world. A world that existed in parallel to the one crumbling around us, a refuge neither of us was ready to abandon despite the dangers gathering on the horizon.

By December, news from Germany had grown so grim that even our most optimistic customers spoke in hushed, worried tones. David received word that his aunt and uncle had disappeared from their Berlin home, their shop seized, their apartment given to a Nazi party official. His parents, already stretched thin supporting relatives who had fled to the Netherlands, fell into a deep despair.

"We should have decided about America months ago," David said one night, pacing our small shared landing. "Now the wait for visas is over a year. Maybe longer."

I had no words of comfort to offer. The window for escape seemed to be closing, and neither of us knew what to do.

On New Year's Eve, with 1939 just hours away, Meneer de Vries invited us to share a simple meal in his apartment above the shop. He opened a bottle of wine he had been saving for a special occasion, poured three glasses, and raised his in a toast.

"To survival," he said simply.

We drank in silence, each lost in private thoughts about what the coming year might bring. Outside, distant celebrations could be heard—music, laughter, the occasional firecracker. The sounds of people determined to find joy despite everything, to believe in a future worth celebrating.

As midnight approached, Meneer de Vries excused himself, claiming fatigue, though I suspected he simply wanted to give David and me a moment alone. We stood by his small window, watching the faint glow of fireworks over the city.

"Whatever happens," David said softly, his fingers interlacing with mine, "we face it together. Yes?"

I squeezed his hand, my heart full of a love I could never adequately express, a fear I could never fully suppress. "Together," I promised.

The clock struck twelve. A new year began—1939. Nine months before the world would change forever. Nine months of borrowed time that we didn't yet know was running out.

David kissed me as distant bells rang across Rotterdam, his lips warm and alive against mine. In that moment, despite everything, I allowed myself to hope. For us. For a future. For a world where our secrets wouldn't have to remain hidden.

It was the last truly peaceful moment we would know for a very long time.

CHAPTER 4: STORM CLOUDS

Rotterdam, 1939

Spring came reluctantly to Rotterdam in 1939. Winter seemed determined to maintain its grip, with icy winds sweeping in from the North Sea well into April. The dampness crept into everything—into the walls of buildings, into bones, into spirits. In the bakery, we fought it with the constant heat of our ovens, but beyond our warm sanctuary, the cold lingered like a premonition.

By May, when the weather finally softened, the city exhaled a collective breath of relief. People spilled into the streets on the first truly warm Sunday, faces tilted toward the sun as if they'd forgotten its feel during the long, dark months. The outdoor cafés filled, couples strolled along the Maas, and children played in parks that had been empty save for crows just weeks before.

David and I spent that Sunday walking through the city, careful to maintain a respectable distance between us in public while savouring the simple pleasure of being outside together. The Rotterdam we moved through that day seemed almost normal—vibrant, busy, alive with possibility. If you didn't look too closely, you could almost believe that nothing had changed, that nothing would change.

But the evidence was there for those willing to see it.

The queue outside the American consulate that stretched around the block, people clutching papers and photographs, their faces etched with quiet desperation. The increased military presence, young Dutch soldiers in crisp uniforms patrolling streets that had never needed such protection before. The whispered conversations that paused when strangers approached, then resumed with glances over shoulders. The newspaper headlines that grew more alarming each day, announcing territorial demands, failed negotiations, troops amassing at borders.

"Look at them," David murmured as we passed a group of university students debating loudly at a café table, their voices carrying across the square. "Still arguing politics as if it's all theoretical. As if it won't touch them."

I followed his gaze, noting the animated gestures, the casual sips of beer between impassioned points. "Maybe it won't," I said, though I didn't believe it.

David's mouth tightened. "It always does, in the end. That's what no one understands until it's too late." His German accent, usually softened after his years in Rotterdam, emerged more strongly when he was upset, giving his words a sharp edge. "We're all connected. What happens in Berlin or Warsaw will happen here too, eventually."

I wanted to disagree, to offer some comforting platitude about Dutch neutrality or the levelheadedness of our government. But the words wouldn't come. Instead, I guided us toward the river, away from the students and their illusion of safety.

At the waterfront, we watched ships move slowly along the Maas, carrying goods in and out of Europe's busiest port. Rotterdam's lifeblood. The sight had always calmed me—the steady rhythm of commerce, the continual movement, the sense of connection to a wider world. Now, I found myself wondering how long it would continue uninterrupted.

"My parents received a letter yesterday," David said quietly, his eyes fixed on a cargo vessel flying a German flag. "From my cousin Ruth in Warsaw. She said Jewish families there are sleeping fully clothed, with small bags packed by their beds. Just in case."

I swallowed hard, trying to imagine such a life—waiting each night for the knock that would force you to flee, if you were lucky enough to have warning at all. "In case of what?"

"In case of whatever comes next." David turned to me, his amber eyes serious in the late afternoon light. "They're expecting something, Arthijs. Everyone is. The only question is when."

That night, lying in my narrow bed with David's breathing steady beside me, I stared at the ceiling and admitted to myself what I had been avoiding for months: war was coming. Not just somewhere distant, but here. To Rotterdam. To us. The thought sat like a stone in my chest, heavy and cold.

I turned toward David, studying his profile in the dim light. The straight line of his nose, the slight furrow between his brows that remained even in sleep, the curve of his lips that could transform so quickly from serious to smiling. I tried to memorise every detail, suddenly afraid that this—his sleeping face, our small room, the quiet intimacy we had created—might not last much longer.

The fear of war became a constant companion that summer. It lurked behind everyday conversations, surfaced in the rising prices at markets, materialised in the government pamphlets about blackout procedures and emergency responses that began appearing in public buildings. Yet alongside the fear, a strange kind of denial persisted—a determined continuation of normal life, as if by clinging to routine, disaster could be prevented.

The bakery remained busy. People still needed bread, perhaps needed the comfort of it more than ever. Our regular customers still came at their usual times, still chatted about the weather or complained about the price of butter. But new topics crept into their conversations: which countries might still accept refugees, which border crossings remained open, which officials might be bribed for exit papers.

Meneer de Vries, usually so stoic, developed a nervous habit of checking the street whenever the shop door opened. He began closing earlier, opening later, as if trying to minimise our exposure to the outside world. He spoke less, thought more, his amber eyes growing distant during quiet moments in the bakery.

In July, he called us into his office after closing. He looked tired, the lines around his eyes deeper than I'd ever seen them.

"I've been in touch with my cousin in America again," he said without preamble. "The situation with visas has worsened. The Americans have tightened their quotas." He paused, choosing his words carefully. "But there may be another option. Switzerland. I have friends in Zurich who own a bakery. They could use help, and Switzerland is likely to remain neutral if..." He didn't finish the sentence. He didn't need to.

David leaned forward. "Both of us?"

Meneer de Vries nodded. "Both of you. Together." He slid a folder across his desk. "I've gathered information. Routes, contacts, the papers you would need. It won't be simple, but it's possible. Think about it."

Later, in the privacy of David's room, we pored over the contents of the folder. Maps, letters of introduction, details about Swiss work permits, transportation schedules. Meneer de Vries had been planning this for months, it seemed, quietly creating an escape route while we continued our daily work.

"We should go," David said, his finger tracing the rail line that would take us from Rotterdam to the Swiss border. "Before it's too late."

I stared at the map, at the countries we would need to cross—the Netherlands, Belgium, France, then finally Switzerland. Countries that might soon be at war. "And leave everything behind? The bakery? Meneer de Vries? My family?"

David looked up, his expression pained. "If we wait too long, we might not have a choice about leaving. Or about staying together."

He was right, and I knew it. But something in me resisted, still unable to fully believe that our world could collapse so completely. "Let's wait a little longer," I said. "See what happens. Maybe things will improve."

David didn't argue, but his silence contained his disagreement. He carefully returned the papers to the folder, his movements measured, controlled. When he finally spoke, his voice was quiet. "I'm afraid, Arthijs. Not just of what might happen to us, but of what I might become if I'm truly afraid. I don't know if I have the courage for what's coming."

I moved to him then, wrapping my arms around him, feeling the tension in his shoulders. "You're the bravest person I know," I whispered against his hair. "Whatever happens, we'll face it together. Remember?"

He nodded against my chest, but neither of us was comforted. The promise, so earnest when we'd made it on New Year's Eve, now seemed fragile in the face of what was unfolding across Europe.

August brought heat that settled over Rotterdam like a blanket, heavy and oppressive. The city moved slowly, as if the weight of the summer and the future pressed equally upon it. News from Poland grew increasingly alarming—border incidents, accusations, threats. The word "inevitable" appeared in newspaper headlines with disturbing frequency.

In the bakery, we worked in a kind of trance, our bodies moving through familiar routines while our minds circled the same questions: When? How bad? What will we do? We spoke less, both to customers and to each other, as if saving our words for when they would truly be needed.

One particularly stifling afternoon, with the shop empty between the lunch and evening rushes, Meneer de Vries surprised us by pulling three glasses and a bottle of jenever from beneath the counter.

"Just one," he said as he poured the clear liquid, his expression unreadable. "For courage."

We each took a glass, the strong juniper scent cutting through the bakery's usual aromas of yeast and sugar.

"To Rotterdam," Meneer de Vries said, raising his glass. "To this place that has been good to us."

The toast felt ominous, like a goodbye. We drank, the jenever burning a path down my throat, settling warm in my stomach. For a moment, none of us spoke, lost in private thoughts about what was to come.

Then David broke the silence, his voice steady despite the emotion I could see in his eyes. "Whatever happens, I want you both to know..." He paused, swallowing hard. "These years here, with you, have been the best of my life."

Meneer de Vries reached out, placing a weathered hand on David's shoulder. "And there will be more good years," he said firmly. "For all of us. This storm will pass, like all storms."

I wanted desperately to believe him. To believe that the world we had built—this bakery, our little family of three, the quiet happiness David and I had found together—could survive what was coming. But the weight in my chest had grown heavier with each passing day, a dread I couldn't shake no matter how I tried.

September 1st dawned clear and mild, a perfect late summer day. We were in the bakery before sunrise, as always, the familiar rhythm of our work a temporary distraction from the tension that had built throughout the week. I was shaping loaves, my hands moving automatically through the motions they knew so well, when Meneer de Vries entered from the street, his face ashen.

"It's happened," he said simply. "Germany has invaded Poland."

The dough beneath my fingers suddenly felt foreign, my hands no longer my own. Beside me, David went completely still, a statue of flour and flesh.

"The radio says Britain and France will declare war if German troops aren't withdrawn within two days," Meneer de Vries continued, his voice unnaturally calm. "But they won't withdraw. Everyone knows that."

We stood in silence, the three of us, absorbing the news that, despite being expected for months, still landed like a physical blow. The world had changed while we kneaded dough and fired ovens, while we weighed flour and counted change. The carefully maintained illusion of normalcy had finally shattered.

That evening, after a day spent serving bread to customers who spoke of nothing but the invasion, David and I sat on the rooftop outside our attic rooms. The city spread before us, its buildings catching the last light of the setting sun. Rotterdam looked peaceful from this height, its wartime preparations invisible, its fears momentarily hidden.

"We should leave," David said, breaking a long silence. "Go to Switzerland, like Meneer de Vries suggested. Or try for England. Anywhere but here."

I knew he was right. It was the only rational choice. Europe was now at war, and two Jewish men—one of them German—would find no safety in its path. And yet, I hesitated.

"I've never been anywhere else," I said softly, gesturing toward the city below. "This is home. Everything I know is here."

"Home can be where we make it," David countered, his voice gentle but insistent. "Together."

I closed my eyes, feeling torn between the safety of the familiar and the necessity of flight. Between my identity as a Rotterdammer, rooted in this city's soil, and my identity as a Jewish man who loved another man—identities that might soon make this home uninhabitable.

"And what about your family?" I asked, opening my eyes to look at him. "Your parents? Your sister? Would we leave them behind?"

David's face tightened with pain. "I don't know," he admitted. "I've been trying to convince them to leave for months. But my father won't abandon his business, and my mother won't leave without him. My sister..." He shook his head. "She believes the Dutch government will protect us. That nothing like Germany can happen here."

Many shared his sister's belief. The Netherlands had remained neutral during the Great War, after all. Our queen was respected, our military small but determined, our borders defensible with strategic flooding if necessary. Surely, the thinking went, the Germans would bypass us as they had before, focusing on their ancient enemies—France and Britain.

Yet even as people voiced these reassurances, preparations for the alternative continued. Sandbags appeared around government buildings. Evacuation routes were published in newspapers. Military leaves were cancelled, reservists called up. Actions that spoke louder than words of neutrality and safety.

In the Jewish quarter, the mood oscillated between optimism and terror. Some families left—for England, for America, for Palestine, for anywhere that would take them. Others dug in, insisting that the Netherlands was different, that Dutch Jews had been integrated into society for centuries, that antisemitism had never taken root here as it had in Germany or Poland.

David and I existed in a strange limbo, neither fully committing to escape nor entirely believing in the possibility of safety. We updated our passports. We set aside a portion of each pay packet for emergency funds. We memorised the routes Meneer de Vries had mapped out. But we did not leave.

The reasons were complex, a tangle of practical concerns and emotional attachments. My aging parents, who refused to even discuss leaving Rotterdam. David's family, caught in the same paralysis of indecision. Meneer de Vries, who would not abandon his bakery. The simple fact that leaving required money we didn't have enough of, connections we didn't possess, luck we couldn't count on.

And beneath all these reasons, a deeper truth I barely admitted to myself: I was afraid. Not just of the journey or of the war, but of what awaited us if we did escape. In Rotterdam, despite everything, we had created a life. We had Meneer de Vries's quiet acceptance. We had the bakery, where our skills were valued. We had a community that knew us, if not the whole truth about us.

Elsewhere, we would be strangers—Jewish refugees in a world increasingly hostile to both Jews and refugees. Our relationship would have no protection, not even the limited safety of familiar surroundings and established routines. We would be exposed, vulnerable in new ways.

So we stayed, watching autumn arrive in a city holding its breath. The leaves turned and fell. The days grew shorter. The news from Poland became unbearable—cities destroyed, civilians massacred, Jews herded into ghettos. Each report reinforced what we already knew: this was not a conventional war. Something darker was unfolding.

David withdrew into himself, speaking less, smiling rarely. At night, he would sometimes cry out in his sleep, words in German I couldn't understand but whose meaning was clear from the anguish in his voice. During the day, he worked mechanically, his natural grace replaced by movements that seemed disconnected from his thoughts.

I worried for him constantly, tried to reach him in the ways I knew how—small touches when no one was looking, favourite foods prepared with special care, quiet conversations in the safety of our rooms. Sometimes he would respond, the David I knew briefly resurfacing. But increasingly, he seemed to be preparing himself for something—a separation, a loss, a transformation—that I couldn't fully comprehend.

In November, the first food rationing began. Sugar, then coffee, then meat. The bakery adjusted, developing recipes that used less of the restricted ingredients. Our customers adapted without much complaint, grateful that bread, at least, remained relatively plentiful.

Winter descended early, with bitter winds and heavy snows that transformed Rotterdam into a monochrome landscape of white and grey. The cold seemed to seep into the city's spirit, freezing hope along with the canals. People moved quickly through the streets, heads down, conserving warmth and energy. Conversations grew shorter, laughter rarer.

Christmas came and went with subdued celebrations. Dutch families maintained their traditions as best they could, but the spectre of what was happening elsewhere in Europe—the countries already occupied, the battles already fought—cast a shadow over even the brightest holiday lights.

News from the front remained distant and confused. The predicted German offensive against France and Britain hadn't materialised. The war seemed to be holding its breath, a pause that some optimistically called the "Phony War" and others, more prescient, recognised as the calm before a storm.

On New Year's Eve, as 1939 prepared to yield to 1940, Meneer de Vries again invited us to share a simple meal in his apartment. Unlike the previous year, there was no special bottle of wine, no attempt at celebration. Just bread, cheese, and soup, shared in quiet companionship.

As midnight approached, Meneer de Vries broke the comfortable silence. "I've been thinking," he said, his amber eyes moving between David and me. "About the bakery. About the future."

We waited, sensing the importance of what was coming.

"If—when—things become worse," he continued carefully, "I want you both to know that this place will always be yours as much as mine. Whatever happens, I consider you my family. My sons." His voice caught slightly on the last word, an unusual display of emotion from such a reserved man.

David reached across the table, grasping Meneer de Vries's flour-roughened hand. "And you are our family," he said simply.

I couldn't speak; my throat tight with feelings I had no words for. Instead, I nodded, hoping Meneer de Vries could read in my face what I couldn't express aloud—gratitude, love, the deep bond that had formed between the three of us over years of shared work and shared secrets.

When the clock struck midnight, we sat in silence, each lost in private thoughts about the year to come. No embraces, no kisses, no declarations. Just three men, connected by something stronger than blood or tradition, facing an uncertain future together.

Outside, Rotterdam greeted 1940 quietly, the usual New Year's celebrations muted by wartime restrictions and the weight of collective anxiety. The fireworks that normally filled the sky were absent, replaced by a stillness that seemed to hold its own warning.

Later, as David and I prepared for bed in the cold attic, he paused by the small window, looking out at the darkened city. "Do you ever wonder who you might have been, in a different world?" he asked softly. "Who we might have been together?"

I moved to stand beside him, our shoulders touching. "Sometimes," I admitted. "But then I think—we found each other in this world, despite everything. That has to count for something."

He turned to me, his face half in shadow, half illuminated by the faint moonlight filtering through the window. "It counts for everything," he said, and kissed me with a tenderness that felt like both a beginning and an ending.

That night, I dreamed of bread. Not the artful loaves we created each day in the bakery, but simple, crude rounds, hastily shaped and poorly fired. In the dream, I was running, these misshapen loaves clutched to my chest, searching for someone—David, I knew, though I never saw his face. The buildings around me were unfamiliar, half-destroyed, smoke rising from their shells. The air tasted of ash and fear.

I woke gasping, my heart racing, the dream clinging to me like smoke to clothing. Beside me, David slept peacefully for once, his breathing deep and regular. I watched him for a long time, memorizing the gentle rise and fall of his chest, the way his hair fell across his forehead, the slight part of his lips.

Whatever came in 1940, I knew with sudden, painful clarity that it would transform us. That the people we had been—the baker's apprentice from Rotterdam, the refugee from Berlin, the two young men who had found unexpected love in a world determined to deny it—might not survive the storm on the horizon.

What remained to be seen was who we might become instead.

CHAPTER 5: THE ROTTERDAM BLITZ

May 14, 1940

I smelled the fire before I saw the flames.

On the morning of May 14, 1940, Rotterdam was already a city under siege. For four days, we had lived in a strange purgatory—neither fully at war nor at peace. The German invasion had begun on May 10th, their planes sweeping over our borders at dawn, their paratroopers dropping from the sky like deadly seeds. Dutch resistance had been brave but futile. By the third day, most of the country had fallen.

Rotterdam, however, remained contested—the Dutch military holding a portion of the city, struggling to protect the vital bridges across the Maas. From our bakery on the north side, we could hear the distant crack of rifles, the occasional explosion. But life continued in a distorted version of normalcy. People still needed to eat. Bread was even more precious in crisis than in peace.

So we baked. Each morning before dawn, David, Meneer de Vries, and I would slip through the quiet streets to open the bakery. We worked in near silence, our hands moving through familiar motions while our minds tracked the approaching danger. Each loaf felt like a small act of defiance. Each customer who braved the streets to buy our bread became a fellow conspirator in the pretence that life could go on.

That morning—Tuesday, the 14th—dawned unusually beautiful after days of misty rain. The sky cleared to a perfect, unblemished blue. In the first light, I stood at our attic window watching golden sunlight illuminate the city's familiar spires and rooftops. Rotterdam looked peaceful, almost defiant in its beauty.

"It looks like nothing could touch it," David said softly, coming to stand beside me.

I nodded, not trusting myself to speak. Over the past days, I had developed a strange superstition—that voicing any hope might destroy it, that naming any fear might summon it.

We dressed quickly and descended to the bakery. Meneer de Vries was already there, his broad back bent over the worktable as he weighed flour. He looked up as we entered, his amber eyes tired but alert.

"The radio says negotiations have begun," he said without preamble. "The Germans have offered terms for surrender."

David and I exchanged glances. Hope and dread mingled in equal measure.

"What terms?" David asked.

Meneer de Vries shrugged. "The usual. Complete capitulation. But it means they might not destroy the city." He turned back to his work. "So we bake. People will need bread, whatever happens."

We fell into our routine—stoking the ovens, mixing dough, shaping loaves. The rhythm was comforting, a counterpoint to the tension humming through the city. Through the front windows, I could see people hurrying past, some carrying suitcases or bags, others empty-handed but moving with purpose. A military truck rumbled by, loaded with soldiers. Their young faces looked grim, determined.

By mid-morning, we had produced our first batches. The scent of fresh bread filled the bakery, a familiar, reassuring smell that momentarily masked the undertone of fear. We opened the doors, and customers trickled in—fewer than normal, but steady. Most bought more than usual, stocking up against uncertainty. We didn't turn anyone away, even when our supplies began to dwindle.

Just before noon, as I was retrieving more flour from the storeroom, I heard it—a distant drone that quickly grew louder. Aircraft engines, dozens of them, approaching from the south.

I froze, the sack half-lifted in my arms. The sound was different from the sporadic planes we'd heard over the past days. This was heavier, more ominous. A swarm rather than individual insects.

The air-raid sirens began to wail.

I dropped the flour and ran to the front of the bakery. David was already at the door, his face pale as he looked up at the sky. Meneer de Vries was ushering the last customers toward the exit.

"Basement," he said tersely as he locked the door. "Now."

We had prepared for this possibility. The small cellar beneath the bakery had been stocked with water, blankets, a radio. Not that any of it would matter if a direct hit came, but it offered some illusion of safety.

As we hurried toward the back stairs, the first explosion shook the building—not close, but near enough to rattle the windows and send a fine shower of plaster dust from the ceiling. Then another, closer. And another.

They're bombing the city centre, I thought numbly. Not just military targets. Everything.

We had just reached the storeroom when the world erupted.

The blast lifted me off my feet and threw me against the far wall. Pain flared through my shoulder and head. The air was suddenly thick with dust and the acrid smell of explosives. My ears rang, making the continuing explosions sound distant, unreal.

I pushed myself up, disoriented. The storeroom was transformed—the back wall partially collapsed, shelves overturned, flour and sugar spilled across the floor like snow. Through the haze, I could make out David's form, crumpled near the doorway. Blood trickled from a cut on his forehead, vividly red against his pale skin.

"David!" I crawled to him, my body protesting every movement. He was breathing, unconscious but alive. I touched his face, leaving smears of flour and blood. "David, wake up. We have to get to the basement."

His eyelids fluttered. "Arthijs?" His voice was slurred, confused.

"Can you stand? We have to move." The bombing continued, a hellish percussion that seemed to be moving closer, methodically destroying the city block by block.

David nodded weakly. I helped him to his feet, supporting him as we staggered toward the cellar door. Only then did I realise—

"Where's Meneer de Vries?"

David's eyes widened. "He was right behind me..."

We turned back, scanning the dust-filled storeroom. Nothing. The doorway to the bakery itself was partially blocked by fallen beams, but there was enough space to squeeze through.

"Wait here," I told David, propping him against the wall. "I'll find him."

Before he could protest, I pushed through the gap into what remained of the bakery.

The front of the shop was gone. Simply gone. Where the counter, display cases, and front window had been was now open air, looking out onto a street transformed into a vision of hell. Buildings across the way were burning, flames leaping from windows. Debris littered the cobblestones. A water pipe had burst somewhere, sending a stream across the wreckage.

And there, beneath a fallen section of our own roof, I saw a hand. Familiar, strong, dusted with flour even now.

"No. No, no, no." I scrambled over broken furniture and chunks of masonry, heedless of the glass cutting into my palms. "Meneer de Vries!"

He was pinned beneath a heavy wooden beam, his lower body crushed. His eyes were open, aware, filled with pain but also a strange calm.

"Arthijs." His voice was barely audible above the ongoing bombardment. "You need to go."

"I'll get you out," I insisted, tugging futilely at the beam. It didn't budge. "David and I together, we can lift it."

He shook his head slightly. "No. Listen to me." He reached for my hand, his grip surprisingly strong. "Take David and go. Now. Through the back. Get to the river if you can."

"I'm not leaving you." Tears cut tracks through the dust on my face.

"You must." Something in his voice—a certainty, an authority—made me pause. "There's nothing you can do for me. But you can save yourselves."

Another explosion rocked what remained of the building. A section of wall collapsed inward, barely missing us. The air grew thicker with dust and smoke.

"Meneer de Vries, please—"

"Noah," he interrupted. "My name is Noah. And you..." His breath hitched with pain. "You are the son I never had. Both of you. Now go. Live." His hand tightened on mine once more, then released. "Go."

I knelt there, paralyzed by grief and indecision. The rational part of me knew he was right—the beam was too heavy, his injuries too severe. But leaving him felt impossible, a betrayal of everything he had done for us.

"I'll come back," I promised, knowing it was likely a lie.

He smiled slightly, his amber eyes holding mine. "I know." Then, with effort, "The papers. For Switzerland. In my desk. Top drawer."

Another blast, closer still. The remaining walls groaned.

"Go," he whispered.

I bent and pressed my lips to his forehead—a son's goodbye to a father—then forced myself to turn away. To leave him there, dying in the ruins of the place he had made a home for all of us.

I found David half-conscious where I'd left him. The dust was so thick now that I could barely see, barely breathe. Every inhalation scraped my lungs.

"Meneer de Vries?" David asked as I pulled him to his feet.

I shook my head, not trusting myself to speak. Understanding darkened his eyes, followed quickly by the same grief that was threatening to overwhelm me.

"We have to go," I managed. "Now. Through the back door."

Together, we stumbled through the storeroom to the rear exit that opened onto a small alley. The door was jammed, swollen in its frame from the concussive force of the bombs. I threw my shoulder against it again and again until it finally gave way, spilling us into the alley.

Outside was chaos. The noon sky had vanished, replaced by a churning canopy of smoke and ash through which the sun appeared as a dim orange disk. The air vibrated with the drone of aircraft, the crash of bombs, the more distant crack of anti-aircraft fire.

We moved as quickly as David's condition allowed, keeping to side streets, heading instinctively toward the river. Others had the same idea—a stream of shell-shocked citizens flowing toward the water, away from the worst of the bombing. Many were injured, bleeding from cuts or burns. Some carried children or supported elderly relatives. All wore the same expression of stunned disbelief.

The Rotterdam we had known was disappearing before our eyes. Each street we turned onto revealed new devastation—historic buildings reduced to rubble, fires consuming entire blocks, roads cratered and impassable. The city that had been my only home, that had seen my first steps and first loves, was dying around us.

As we neared the Maas, the crowd thickened. People clustered along the waterfront, as if proximity to the river might offer some protection. The bridges were packed with those trying to flee to the south bank, where the bombing seemed less intense.

I looked back at the city centre and felt my heart stop. Where Rotterdam's distinctive skyline had stood that morning was now a roiling mass of smoke and flame. The church spires, the clock tower, the elegant facades of centuries-old buildings—all gone or going. The methodical destruction was unlike anything I had imagined in even my worst fears.

"This isn't war," David murmured beside me, his voice hollow. "This is annihilation."

I couldn't answer. Words seemed inadequate, almost obscene in the face of such wholesale destruction.

A fresh wave of bombers appeared overhead, their dark shapes visible through gaps in the smoke. The crowd along the riverbank surged with renewed panic.

"We need shelter," I said, pulling David away from the exposed quayside. My eyes scanned the nearby buildings, most of which were damaged but still standing. "There."

I pointed to a warehouse about a hundred meters down the riverfront. Its massive stone walls had withstood the bombing better than the surrounding structures. The main doors stood open, and I could see people taking refuge inside.

We were halfway there when the next wave of bombs fell.

The world became noise and pressure and heat. The ground heaved beneath our feet. I was vaguely aware of falling, of David's hand being torn from mine. Then nothing.

I came back to consciousness slowly, my senses returning one by one. First touch—rough stone beneath my cheek, something warm and wet running down my face. Then smell—smoke, dust, the copper tang of blood. Then hearing—not the sharp explosions of before, but a continuous roar punctuated by human cries. Finally sight—a world transformed into a monochrome hell of grey and orange.

I pushed myself up, ignoring the protests from my battered body. "David?" My voice was a croak, barely audible even to myself. "David!"

Moving was agony. My right leg buckled when I tried to stand, forcing me to crawl through debris. All around me, others were doing the same—dragging themselves from the wreckage, calling out for loved ones, helping those who couldn't move on their own.

A hand grabbed my shoulder. I turned, hope flaring, but it wasn't David. A stranger, an older man with blood streaming from a gash across his scalp.

"The warehouse," he gasped. "Direct hit. Don't go that way. Nothing left."

My blood ran cold. The warehouse we had been heading for. Had David reached it before me?

"A man," I said desperately. "Dark hair, my age. Have you seen him?"

The man shook his head and moved on, calling a woman's name.

I continued my frantic search, combing the riverbank in an expanding radius from where I'd fallen. The bombing had stopped, though fires still raged throughout the city. The air was thick with heat and ash, making breathing difficult, visibility poor. My voice grew hoarser as I called David's name over and over.

Hours passed. The sun began to set, though it was hard to tell through the pall of smoke that hung over Rotterdam. Emergency workers appeared, moving through the rubble, pulling out survivors and covering the dead with whatever was at hand. I joined them, helping where I could, always searching, always listening for David's voice, his laugh, anything.

As darkness fell, the true scope of the destruction became even more apparent. The fires illuminated a cityscape transformed beyond recognition. Where the heart of Rotterdam had stood that morning was now a smoking wasteland. The historic centre, the shopping districts, whole residential neighbourhoods—gone. Centuries of history and thousands of lives extinguished in a single afternoon.

I found myself back at the river's edge as midnight approached, exhaustion finally overcoming my desperate search. My body was a catalogue of pain—cuts, bruises, a possible broken rib. But the physical agony was nothing compared to the hollow ache in my chest.

David was gone. Meneer de Vries—Noah—was gone. The bakery was gone. Everything that had anchored my life had been destroyed in a few hours of mechanised terror.

I sat on a chunk of broken wall, watching the fires reflect in the dark waters of the Maas. For the first time since the bombing began, I allowed myself to fully feel the grief that had been building since I'd seen Noah's hand protruding from the rubble. Tears came, then racking sobs that tore at my injured ribs. I wept for him, for David, for our city, for the future we'd never have.

When the tears finally subsided, I was empty. Hollowed out. Too exhausted even for fear or further grief. I stared at the water, wondering dully what would happen next. Where I would go. How I would live.

"Are you injured?" A voice beside me made me start. A nurse, her uniform stained with blood and soot, her young face lined with fatigue beyond her years.

"No," I lied automatically. "Others need help more."

She studied me for a moment, her expression softening. "You've lost someone."

It wasn't a question. How many others had she seen today, wearing the same stunned expression, the same grief etched into their faces?

"Everyone," I whispered.

She nodded, understanding without needing details. "The emergency station is two blocks that way. Food, water, medical treatment." She pressed something into my hand—a small packet of bandages. "For your head. The cut needs cleaning."

Then she was gone, moving on to the next survivor.

I turned the packet over in my hands, oddly touched by this small act of kindness amidst such overwhelming destruction. It anchored me somehow, reminded me that humanity persisted even here, even now.

With effort, I stood, wincing as my injured leg took my weight. The nurse was right—I needed water, food, proper medical attention. I needed to survive this night, to face whatever came after. I owed that much to Noah, to David. To remember them. To live, as Noah had commanded with his dying breath.

I began limping in the direction the nurse had indicated, each step a negotiation with pain. Around me, other survivors moved with similar slowness, similarly wounded in body and spirit. We formed a ragged procession through streets rendered unfamiliar by destruction.

Somewhere in the distance, I could hear the whine of aircraft returning—reconnaissance planes, perhaps, or a final bomber run to complete the obliteration. I didn't quicken my pace. Whatever came next would come, whether I hurried or not.

As I walked, memories of the morning surfaced—David beside me at the window, the perfect blue sky, the routine comfort of baking bread. How quickly it had all vanished, how thoroughly the world had transformed. I thought of what Noah had said in his final moments—about the papers for Switzerland in his desk. A plan we had delayed too long, a future now doubly impossible without David.

Yet something in me refused to fully accept that David was gone. Perhaps it was denial, the first stage of grief. Perhaps it was a lover's irrational hope. But I couldn't—wouldn't—believe he had perished without my knowing it, without my feeling that severing in the core of my being.

Dawn found me at the emergency station, a school gymnasium transformed into a makeshift hospital and shelter. I had my head wound cleaned and bandaged, accepted water and a bowl of thin soup. Around me, hundreds of others like me sat in similar states of shock, waiting for news, for direction, for some sense of what came next.

The radio announced that Rotterdam had surrendered. That the entire Netherlands had surrendered. That we were now under German occupation. The words washed over me, important yet somehow distant, as if they referred to another life, another person.

All that mattered was finding David. And if not finding him living, then at least knowing for certain that he was gone. I needed that closure, that terrible certainty, before I could think about survival.

As the first light of May 15th strengthened, I left the gymnasium and made my way back toward the ruins of the bakery. I had to see it once more. Had to confirm that nothing remained. Had to say goodbye properly to the place that had been my true home.

The destruction seemed even worse in daylight. Buildings I had known all my life were simply gone, leaving gaps in the streetscape like missing teeth. The air still tasted of ash and chemicals, though the fires had mostly burned themselves out. Here and there, rescue workers continued to dig through collapsed structures, their hopes of finding survivors dwindling with each hour that passed.

When I reached the street where the bakery had stood, I almost walked past it. The buildings on either side were damaged but recognizable; the bakery itself was a crater, a hole in the fabric of the city. Nothing remained of the shop, the storeroom, our attic rooms. Nothing to suggest the life that had flourished there just hours before.

I stood at the edge of the rubble, unable to step onto what felt like a grave. Somewhere beneath those broken stones and shattered beams lay Noah de Vries, the man who had shaped me as surely as I had shaped dough under his guidance. The man who had given me a home, a trade, a family when I had needed all three.

"I'll remember," I promised quietly. "Everything you taught me. Everything you were."

It was the only epitaph I could offer.

As I turned to leave, something caught my eye—a glint of metal among the wreckage. I moved closer, careful of my footing on the unstable debris. There, protruding from what might have been the office wall, was the corner of a metal box.

Noah's desk safe.

I scrambled over the rubble, heedless of the broken glass and splintered wood that tore at my hands and knees. The safe was partially exposed, its door hanging open—the force of the explosion had torn it from its hiding place behind the desk and sprung the lock.

Inside was a bundle of papers, miraculously intact. The Switzerland documents, just as Noah had mentioned. Passports. Letters of introduction. Train tickets dated for the following week—a departure Noah had arranged without telling us, perhaps knowing we would never leave otherwise.

And something else. A small leather pouch. I opened it to find a stack of guilders, more money than I had ever seen in one place, and two gold rings on a simple chain.

I clutched the documents and pouch to my chest, overcome by this final gift. Noah had prepared for everything, had tried to ensure our survival even as his city crumbled around him. His foresight, his love, reached out from beyond death, offering a lifeline I had thought severed.

But without David, what use was any of it?

I made my way back to the riverfront, the precious bundle secure inside my shirt. The Maas flowed on, indifferent to the destruction on its banks, carrying debris and ash toward the sea. I watched a charred timber float past, a remnant of someone's home or business.

"I'll find you," I whispered, as if David could hear me across whatever distance separated us. "If you're out there, I'll find you."

It was a promise to him, to myself, to whatever power might be listening. A declaration of intent in a world where intentions seemed suddenly, terribly meaningless.

Rotterdam burned around me, a city transformed in the space of an afternoon from my beloved home into a wasteland of ash and memory. But I was still here. Still breathing. Still hoping, despite everything, for David's survival.

And until I knew for certain, I would search. I would survive. I would remember.

It was all I had left.

CHAPTER 6: AFTERMATH

Summer 1940

The city that emerged from the ashes of May 14th was not Rotterdam.

It wore Rotterdam's name. It occupied Rotterdam's geography. The Maas still flowed through it, indifferent to the catastrophe on its banks. But this hollow skeleton of broken buildings and cratered streets was a stranger to me, as unfamiliar as a foreign country.

In the weeks following the bombing, I wandered through this alien landscape, searching. For David, yes—always for David—but also for something recognizable, some fragment of the world I had lost. I scrutinised every face I passed, every figure huddled in makeshift shelters or queuing for rations. I visited every emergency station, every makeshift hospital, scanning lists of the living and the dead with equal desperation.

David's name appeared on neither.

The Germans established order with brutal efficiency. Within days of the surrender, their vehicles rumbled through streets cleared just enough to allow passage. Their uniforms became a common sight, their harsh language a constant reminder of our new reality. Signs in German appeared alongside Dutch ones. Curfews were announced. Ration cards distributed. Life, such as it was, resumed under occupation.

I existed on the margins of this new order. The small pouch of money Noah had left in his safe allowed me to rent a tiny room in a boarding house that had survived near the harbour. The landlady asked few questions, concerned only with my ability to pay. My injuries from the bombing healed slowly—the cut on my head closing to leave a thin scar above my temple, the bruises on my ribs fading from angry purple to sickly yellow. My body recovered. The rest of me remained fractured, incomplete.

Nights were the worst. In the darkness, memories surfaced with painful clarity—David's laugh, the warmth of his hand in mine, the way sunlight caught in his hair. Noah's voice, steady even in his final moments. The bakery, filled with the scent of fresh bread and the quiet rhythm of our shared work. Dreams would offer cruel reunions, only to dissolve into wakefulness and renewed grief.

By day, I forced myself to continue the search. I walked miles through the devastated city, using landmarks that had survived to orient myself in what had once been familiar neighbourhoods. The Germans had begun demolition of damaged buildings deemed unsalvageable, and crews of Dutch workers were clearing debris, stacking bricks for reuse, salvaging what could be saved. The sound of their labour—pickaxes against stone, the rumble of carts hauling rubble—became the heartbeat of the wounded city.

In early June, I reached what had been the Jewish quarter. The destruction here was particularly complete, whether by cruel design or terrible coincidence. The old synagogue was a roofless shell. Shops where I had bought holiday treats as a child were reduced to rubble. The street where my family had lived was unrecognizable, the row of narrow houses replaced by piles of broken masonry and charred timber.

I stood in what might have been the doorway of my childhood home, trying to feel something—grief, anger, loss. But I was numb, emptied of emotion by the magnitude of the destruction. My family had moved to Zeeland years before, seeking the quiet of the countryside as my father's health declined. They had escaped this particular horror, at least. The letters I had sent after the bombing had gone unanswered, the postal service disrupted by war and occupation. I could only hope they were safe, unaware of what had become of Rotterdam, of what had become of me.

On the edge of what had been the Jewish quarter, I encountered a group of men and women sifting through the ruins of a community centre. They worked systematically, forming a human chain to move debris, occasionally stopping when something salvageable was discovered—a book, a ceremonial object, a photograph. Their faces were grim but determined, unified in purpose despite the hopelessness of their task.

I joined them without a word, taking my place in their chain. No one questioned my presence or my right to help. We worked in near silence, the occasional murmured direction or request for water the only interruption to our labour. As the sun began to set, a middle-aged man with silver at his temples called a halt.

"Enough for today," he said quietly. "We'll continue tomorrow."

As the group dispersed, he approached me. "You're new," he observed, his eyes taking in my dirty clothes, the healing cut on my temple, the hollowness that I knew had overtaken my face. "I'm Joseph Levi."

"Arthijs van Leeuwen," I replied, my voice rough from disuse.

He nodded, as if confirming something to himself. "You were in the bombing."

It wasn't a question, but I answered anyway. "Yes. Near the harbour. The bakery where I worked..." I couldn't finish.

"You're searching for someone," he said, again with that strange certainty.

"My friend. David Cohen. We were separated during the blitz." I swallowed hard. "He's German. Jewish. A refugee."

Joseph's eyes softened with understanding and something like pity. "Come," he said, gesturing toward a building at the corner that had somehow survived relatively intact. "We have soup. Not much, but it's hot."

I hesitated, then followed. The building had been a small grocery store, now repurposed as a community centre for those who remained in the area. Tables had been set up in what had been the main shop, and several large pots steamed on portable stoves. The air smelled of vegetable broth and damp stone.

Joseph led me to a table where a woman was ladling soup into mismatched bowls. She handed me one without comment, her dark eyes taking in my appearance with the same assessing gaze Joseph had used. I nodded my thanks and sat at an empty table, suddenly aware of how hungry I was.

The soup was thin but flavourful—carrots, potatoes, a hint of onion. I ate slowly, savouring the first hot meal I'd had in days. Around me, others did the same, their conversations a low murmur in a mix of Dutch and Yiddish. Here was a pocket of community that had somehow survived the bomb and fire, people coming together in the face of shared loss.

Joseph joined me as I finished, setting a cup of weak tea before me. "You have somewhere to stay?" he asked.

"A room. Near the harbour."

He nodded. "And papers? Identity cards?"

I stiffened. My identity papers had been in the bakery, in the small desk beside my bed. Lost, like everything else.

"No," I admitted.

Joseph leaned closer, his voice dropping. "That's dangerous now. The Germans are already beginning to register Jews. Without papers, you could be arrested, questioned. Or worse."

A chill ran through me. In the chaos following the bombing, I hadn't considered this new vulnerability. Without proof of identity, I existed in a perilous limbo.

"I can help," Joseph continued. "We have people who can create new papers. Not perfect, but enough to keep you safe for now."

"Why would you help me?" I asked, wariness overcoming gratitude. "You don't know me."

Joseph's gaze was steady. "Because we help each other. Because soon, we may have no one else to rely on."

I considered his offer. The papers Noah had secured for Switzerland included a passport—a real one, with my photograph and name—but using it would mean abandoning the search for David. I wasn't ready for that. Not yet.

"There would be a cost," I said carefully.

Joseph's mouth quirked in a small, sad smile. "Of course. Nothing is free, especially now. But not money." He gestured around the makeshift community centre. "We need hands. Strong backs. People willing to help others while helping themselves."

It was a fair exchange. More than fair, in a world where fairness had become a luxury few could afford.

"Alright," I agreed. "What do I do?"

"Come back tomorrow. Early. Bring whatever identification you have, even if it's damaged. A photograph if you have one." He paused. "And I'll ask about your friend. David Cohen. We keep lists."

Hope flickered briefly, a small flame quickly extinguished by experience. How many lists had I already checked, how many names scanned in desperate search?

"Thank you," I said simply.

As promised, I returned the next morning. The community centre was already busy, people coming and going with purposeful energy. Joseph was nowhere to be seen, but the woman who had served soup the previous evening beckoned me to a back room that had once been a storage area. A man sat at a small table, surrounded by papers, rubber stamps, and a camera on a tripod.

"Sit," he instructed, not unkindly. "Joseph explained your situation."

I did as directed, watching as he prepared papers with practiced efficiency. No names were exchanged. No unnecessary questions asked. He took my photograph with a small flash that momentarily blinded me, then continued working while my vision cleared.

"This will identify you as Arthijs van Leeuwen, born in Rotterdam, occupation baker," he explained as he wrote. "Not Jewish. It's safer that way."

I started to protest, some irrational loyalty making me reluctant to deny my heritage, even on paper.

"It's not about shame," the man said, correctly interpreting my hesitation. "It's about survival. The Germans are beginning to impose restrictions on Jews. This will give you freedom of movement. The ability to work. To continue your search."

He had found the one argument that could persuade me.

"These won't withstand serious scrutiny," he continued, applying a stamp to the finished document. "But they're good enough for routine checks. Keep to yourself. Don't draw attention." He looked up, his gaze direct. "And if you find yourself in a situation where they might be examined too closely, destroy them. Better to be detained for lacking papers than for carrying false ones."

He handed me the completed documents—an identity card and a work permit. The photograph showed a face I barely recognised as my own, gaunt and haunted, eyes too large in a thin face. But the papers themselves looked official, with appropriate stamps and signatures.

"Memorise the details," the man advised. "Date of birth. Address. If questioned, answer confidently but briefly. Don't volunteer information."

I nodded, studying the documents carefully. One small lie—the omission of my Jewish identity—that might mean the difference between life and death in this new reality.

"Thank you," I said when I had committed the details to memory.

The man waved away my gratitude. "Joseph says you'll work with the recovery crew. That's payment enough." He began gathering his equipment with the clear implication that our business was concluded.

I found Joseph outside, organizing a group preparing to return to the ruins of the synagogue. He nodded at my approach, wordlessly handing me a pair of work gloves.

"Did you find anything?" I asked as we walked. "About David?"

Joseph's expression was carefully neutral. "His name isn't on our lists. Not among the confirmed dead or the survivors we've documented." He paused. "That could mean many things."

I knew those possibilities all too well. David could have been removed from the city, injured and unidentified in a hospital elsewhere. He could have fled, believing me dead. Or his body could lie still undiscovered beneath the ruins, one of hundreds yet to be recovered.

"I'll keep looking," I said, more to myself than to Joseph.

He clasped my shoulder briefly. "Yes. But for now, we work. It helps."

He was right. The physical labour of clearing debris, of searching for salvageable items, occupied my body and numbed my mind. Each stone moved, each object recovered, became a small act of defiance against destruction. And in the company of others similarly wounded by loss, I found an unexpected community.

Days became weeks. June's warmth gave way to July's heat, unusual for Rotterdam and made more oppressive by the dust that still rose from the ruins. The German occupation solidified, their control extending into every aspect of daily life. New regulations appeared daily, posted on walls and announced through loudspeakers. Curfews tightened. Travel became restricted. Food grew scarcer, the ration system more stringent.

And, as Joseph had warned, the registration of Jews began.

The announcement came in early July—all Jewish residents required to register with German authorities by the end of the month. Special identity cards would be issued, businesses marked, a census taken. The pretence was administrative efficiency, but none of us were fooled. This was the beginning of something darker, a systematic identification of those the Germans considered undesirable.

"Don't register," Joseph advised the evening the announcement was posted. We sat in the back room of the community centre, voices low despite the closed door. "Your papers show you as non-Jewish. Use that protection."

I stared at the rough table surface, conflicted. "It feels like betrayal."

Joseph leaned forward, his voice intense. "Listen to me, Arthijs. This registration isn't about counting us. It's about controlling us. First identification, then restriction, then..." He didn't finish, but he didn't need to. The stories filtering in from Poland and Germany made the progression clear.

"I can't just stop being who I am," I argued.

"No one's asking you to change who you are in your heart," Joseph countered. "Only what you show to them. Think of it as a mask, a necessary deception."

I thought of David, of how careful we had been to hide our true relationship from the world. One secret had already shaped my life; another might now preserve it.

"What about the others?" I gestured vaguely toward the main room, where several families were finishing their evening meal. "They don't have false papers."

Joseph's expression darkened. "Some will register. They believe compliance offers safety, that following rules will protect them. Others will try to hide, to disappear." He sighed, suddenly looking much older than his years. "There's no perfect answer, no guaranteed safety. We each make our choice and hope."

My choice seemed clear, if uncomfortable. The false identity I now carried offered protection that would be foolish to abandon. And if I were to continue searching for David, I needed the freedom this deception provided.

Yet as July progressed and I watched families line up outside German administrative offices, identity documents and family photographs in hand, the weight of my falsehood grew heavier. These were my people, submitting to a process I had avoided through luck and the help of strangers. Their faces as they emerged from registration were a complex mix of relief and fear—relief that the dreaded process was complete, fear of what it might mean for their future.

By the end of July, the registration was largely complete. Those who had complied received new identity cards stamped with a large "J." The next step came swiftly—restrictions on where Jews could work, which businesses they could enter, which parts of the city they could access. The invisible lines dividing Rotterdam's citizens became visible, enforced by law and the threat of punishment.

I continued my search for David, the false papers allowing me to move freely through areas now restricted to those with "J" stamped on their identity cards. I checked hospitals again, refugee centres, lists of those transported to other cities. I asked questions carefully, aware that too much interest might draw unwanted attention.

At night, in my small harbour room, I would take out the documents Noah had prepared for Switzerland—the passport, the letters of introduction, the train tickets now long expired. The gold rings on their simple chain. Tangible reminders of a future we had planned, David and I, a future now suspended in the limbo of uncertainty.

August brought no answers, only increasing hardship. The German authorities tightened their grip on the city. More restrictions, more controls. The reconstruction of Rotterdam proceeded according to their plans, with Dutch labour under German supervision. The rubble was cleared, revealing the full extent of the destruction—nearly eight hundred dead, eighty thousand homeless, the historic heart of the city simply gone.

In its place, a new Rotterdam was beginning to emerge, designed on German drawing boards with wide avenues suitable for military vehicles and stark, utilitarian buildings. This was to be a city rebuilt as a monument to conquest, a daily reminder of power and submission.

I watched this transformation from the margins, still searching, still hoping against reason for some sign of David. But as summer waned and the first hints of autumn appeared in the air, a cold realization was settling over me.

The Rotterdam I had known was gone. David was gone. Noah was gone. And I existed now in a shadow world of false identity and borrowed time, caught between the pull of memory and the push of survival.

One evening in late August, I returned to my harbour room to find the door ajar. Fear prickled along my spine—a break-in was dangerous enough, but the possibility of my false papers being discovered was worse. I approached cautiously, listening for movement inside.

Silence.

I pushed the door open slowly, scanning the small space. Nothing seemed disturbed at first glance. My few possessions remained in their places. No one was there, yet someone had clearly entered. Whether it was a simple mistake by another tenant, a thief who had been scared away, or something more sinister—German authorities making checks—I couldn't know.

I gathered my most important possessions, including my false papers and Noah's documents, and spent the night elsewhere, huddled in an abandoned building near the docks. The next day, I found a new room in a different part of the city.

The incident, minor as it might have been, reinforced what I already knew. In occupied Rotterdam, there was no real safety, no true security. Just the constant vigilance of a hunted man, living on the margins, one misstep away from discovery.

CHAPTER 7: THE GERMAN SOLDIER

Autumn 1940

Rotterdam was no longer my city.

In the months after the bombing, a new order had settled over the ruins. The Germans moved through the streets as if they had always belonged there, their boots echoing on cobblestones where I had once walked freely. The destruction of May had given way to a controlled demolition—the methodical dismantling of what remained of the old city to make way for their vision of the new.

The uniform I had found on my bed haunted me. I had fled the room immediately, not daring to return for several days. When I finally did, the uniform was gone, as if it had never existed. Perhaps it hadn't—perhaps grief and exhaustion had conjured a phantom, a manifestation of my deepest fears. But I knew better. Someone had found me. Someone knew where I slept.

I moved again, abandoning the harbour room for a small attic space in a house near what remained of the Jewish quarter. The elderly widow who owned it asked no questions when I offered a month's rent in advance. Her eyes, clouded with cataracts, barely registered my face. She simply took the money and showed me the narrow stairs to my new shelter.

September brought colder weather and new restrictions. The German authorities announced that all Jews must now wear a yellow star on their outer clothing when in public. The stars—a mockery of the Star of David—were distributed through the registration offices, to be sewn onto coats and jackets. "JOD," they proclaimed in black letters. Jew.

I watched from the shadows as people emerged from the distribution centres, the bright yellow badges clutched in their hands, faces tight with humiliation and fear. Many sewed them on immediately, their fingers working quickly as if to get the dreaded task over with. Others waited until they were home, prolonging their last hours of unmarked existence.

I had been spared this particular degradation by my false papers, but the sight of those stars—bright against dark clothing, impossible to miss, deliberately so—filled me with a cold rage. This was not about identification. This was about marking. Separating. Making visible what had once been private.

I thought of David, of how we had hidden a different kind of identity, of how careful we had been to pass as merely friends in public. Now, an essential part of who we were—our Jewish heritage—was to be displayed for all to see, made into a target.

If he was still alive, David would now wear that star. The thought was a knife twisting in my chest.

My work with Joseph's recovery crew had ended as the official German cleanup took over. The community centre where we had gathered was closed, its remaining resources confiscated. Joseph himself had disappeared one night in early September, whispers suggesting he had gone into hiding or escaped to the countryside. Others from our group had similarly vanished, sensing what was coming next.

I had nowhere to go, no one to turn to. My parents in Zeeland might as well have been on another continent—travel permits were nearly impossible to obtain, especially for someone with questionable papers. I existed in a kind of limbo, moving through the city like a ghost, searching for a man who might already be a ghost himself.

By October, food had become desperately scarce. The ration system provided barely enough to survive, and the black market prices were beyond what my dwindling funds could afford. I had begun taking whatever work I could find—loading crates at the docks when guards looked the other way, clearing rubble from bombed sites, unloading German supply trucks under the bored gaze of soldiers.

The physical labour kept me warm as the weather turned colder. It exhausted my body enough that sleep sometimes came without nightmares. And it allowed me to continue my search, moving through different parts of the city, watching, listening, hoping for some mention of David.

On a raw October evening, I was returning from a day of work at the docks. My muscles ached, my hands were rough with blisters, and hunger gnawed at my stomach. The sunset painted the sky in shades of amber and rose, colours that reminded me painfully of David's eyes in certain lights. I found myself drawn to the river, to the spot where the Maas widened before flowing toward the sea.

The waterfront was mostly deserted at this hour. A few dock workers hurried homeward before curfew. A pair of German soldiers patrolled in the distance, their silhouettes distinct against the darkening sky. I sat on a stone bollard, watching the water flow past, too tired to continue immediately to my attic room, too hungry to care about the risks of being out as darkness fell.

The river had always calmed me. Even now, after everything, there was solace in its constant movement, its indifference to the human drama playing out on its banks. Water understood time differently than we did. It would be here long after the Germans were gone, long after all of us were gone.

I was so lost in these thoughts that I didn't hear the footsteps approaching until they were nearly upon me. I tensed, ready to flee, then forced myself to relax. My papers were in order—false, but convincing. I wore no yellow star. There was no reason for alarm.

"It's nearly curfew."

The voice was young, male, speaking Dutch with a heavy German accent. I turned slowly to find a soldier standing a few meters away, watching me with a guarded expression.

He was tall and fair, the classic Aryan ideal the Reich so celebrated. His uniform was immaculate, the insignia of a Wehrmacht lieutenant gleaming in the fading light. Yet there was something in his stance—a certain hesitancy, a lack of the arrogance I had come to expect from German officers—that gave me pause.

"I was just leaving," I said, rising to my feet.

The soldier made no move toward me. Instead, he turned slightly to look out over the water. "The river is beautiful at this hour."

The observation was so unexpected, so oddly normal, that I found myself answering without thinking. "Yes. It always has been."

He glanced at me. "You are from Rotterdam?"

I nodded, caution returning. These conversational questions often preceded more pointed ones about identity, employment, purpose.

"Before," he said, gesturing vaguely toward the skyline where buildings had once stood. "What was it like?"

There was something in his voice—a genuine curiosity, perhaps even a hint of regret—that caught me off guard.

"Beautiful," I said after a moment. "Old. The buildings had history. Character." I shouldn't be speaking so freely to a German soldier, but the words came anyway. "The Great Church had bells that rang every hour. You could hear them throughout the city."

The soldier nodded, his gaze still on the river. "Berlin has such bells too. Or did." A small frown creased his forehead. "Everything changes now."

This strange conversation, this moment of almost normal human exchange, felt surreal after months of fear and hiding. I studied him more carefully—his profile sharp against the darkening sky, his hands clasped behind his back in a pose that seemed more contemplative than military.

"You should go," he said suddenly, turning back to me. "Curfew begins soon."

I nodded and took a step toward the street. Then, an impulse I couldn't explain made me ask, "Do you come here often? To the river?"

Something flickered in his pale eyes—surprise, perhaps, that I would continue the conversation. "When I can. It reminds me of home."

"And where is home?"

"A small town near Hamburg. On the Elbe." His mouth quirked in what might have been the ghost of a smile. "Another river."

I should have left then. Should have walked away without another word. Nothing good could come from conversing with a German officer, no matter how seemingly benign. Yet I lingered, drawn by something I couldn't name—a momentary connection, a brief respite from the isolation of my existence.

"I'm Arthijs," I said, immediately regretting the disclosure.

The soldier hesitated, then nodded once. "Fritz. Fritz Neumann."

"Well, Lieutenant Neumann, I'll leave you to your contemplation." I turned to go, eager now to end this strange encounter before it turned dangerous.

"Wait." His voice stopped me. He took a step closer, his expression changing as he examined my face more carefully in the fading light. "Where is your star?"

My blood froze. The star. The yellow badge every Jew was required to wear. How had he known? My papers listed me as non-Jewish. I had been so careful.

"I don't—" I began, but he cut me off with a sharp gesture.

"You are van Leeuwen, yes? From the Jewish quarter?" His voice was low, urgent. "I've seen your name. On a list."

My mind raced. Denial was useless. If he had seen my name on an official list, he knew. The question was what he would do with that knowledge.

"Yes," I admitted, seeing no alternative.

Fritz exhaled, his shoulders dropping. His lips pressed together as if he had just bitten into something sour. Then he shook his head, almost imperceptibly.

"Go home," he said, so quietly I barely heard him. "Before someone else asks."

I swallowed hard, my pulse a hammer in my throat. "You're not going to report me?"

His eyes met mine, and in that moment, I saw something unexpected—conflict, uncertainty, perhaps even fear. "No," he said simply. "Just go."

I didn't need to be told a third time. I turned and walked away, forcing myself not to run, not to look back. Every step, I expected to hear his shout, to feel a hand on my shoulder, to face the consequences of being discovered. But nothing came. Only the sound of my own footsteps and the distant lap of water against stone.

By the time I reached the relative safety of the streets leading to my attic room, my heart had slowed to something approaching normal. But my mind was in turmoil. Why had he let me go? What list had he seen my name on? And most perplexing of all—why had he seemed almost as afraid as I was?

The encounter played over and over in my mind as I climbed the narrow stairs to my room. Lieutenant Fritz Neumann. A German officer who stood by the river missing his home. Who recognised me as Jewish yet allowed me to walk away.

Nothing made sense anymore. The world had become a place where bombs could destroy a city in an afternoon, where wearing a yellow star could mean the difference between life and death, where a German soldier might enforce ruthless laws one moment and show unexpected mercy the next.

I sat on my narrow bed in the darkness, too agitated to light a lamp, too confused to sleep. The memory of Fritz's face—the conflict in his pale eyes, the moment of decision I had witnessed—burned in my mind. There had been something in that look, something beyond the simple interaction of occupied and occupier. A recognition.

Not of me, specifically. He hadn't known me before today. But perhaps a recognition of something in me. Something he understood without words.

The thought was disturbing, unsettling in ways I couldn't articulate even to myself. To imagine any commonality with a man who wore that uniform, who served the regime that had destroyed my city and threatened my people... it felt like betrayal. Of David. Of Noah. Of everything I had lost.

And yet, I couldn't dismiss the moment by the river. The brief, strange connection that had saved me from discovery and possible arrest.

I lay back on the thin mattress, staring up at the ceiling I couldn't see in the darkness. Who was Fritz Neumann? What list had my name been on? And why—the question that kept circling back—why had he let me go?

Sleep eluded me that night, and many nights after. The German soldier by the river had introduced a new uncertainty into my already precarious existence. I avoided the waterfront after that, taking different routes through the city, staying away from areas heavily patrolled by German officers.

Yet I found myself watching for him. In the streets, among the patrols, at checkpoints. Part of me wanted answers to the questions that plagued me. Part of me feared those answers might be worse than the uncertainty.

October yielded to November, bringing shorter days and biting cold. The reconstruction continued, German efficiency transforming the wasteland of May into the beginnings of their new vision for Rotterdam. Buildings rose among the remaining ruins—functional, soulless structures of concrete and steel. The occupiers seemed determined to erase all memory of what had been, to replace the city's character with their own rigid order.

I continued my search for David with decreasing hope. Each day without news, each list checked without finding his name, each rumour followed to a dead end—all steadily eroded my conviction that he had survived. Yet I couldn't stop. To give up the search would be to accept his loss, to consign him to memory rather than possibility. I wasn't ready for that. Not yet.

And through it all, the memory of that encounter by the river lingered. Fritz Neumann, the German soldier who had seen me, truly seen me, and chosen not to report what he found. In a world where every day brought new cruelties, new restrictions, new reasons for despair, that small act of mercy remained inexplicable.

A mystery I both longed and feared to solve.

CHAPTER 8: THE RAID

Winter 1940

Winter fell upon Rotterdam like judgment.

The first snow came in early December, a silent blanket that briefly softened the harsh angles of destruction and reconstruction. For a few hours, the city was transformed—ruins became abstract sculptures, construction sites disappeared beneath pristine white, and the constant dust of demolition was temporarily laid to rest. I stood at my attic window that morning, watching the world turn white, and felt a momentary peace.

But like all beautiful things in occupied Rotterdam, it didn't last. By afternoon, German trucks and boots had churned the snow to grey slush. Construction resumed, the metallic clang of work echoing through streets made narrower by snowbanks. The cold became another enemy to fight, another hardship to endure in a city already overburdened with suffering.

Food grew scarcer as winter deepened. The ration system provided barely enough to survive, and what was available was often of poor quality—bread that crumbled in your hands, vegetables half-rotted, meat so scarce it became a distant memory. I had grown accustomed to the constant companionship of hunger, to the hollow feeling that no amount of watery soup could fill. My body had thinned, my clothes hanging loose where they had once fit properly.

Yet physical hunger was easier to bear than the other hunger—the gnawing need for answers, for certainty about

David's fate. After months of searching, I had begun to accept what I had long feared. If he had survived the bombing, he would have found a way to let me know. He would have searched for me as desperately as I had searched for him. The absence of any trace, any rumour, any sign spoke its own terrible truth.

Still, I couldn't bring myself to fully acknowledge what that meant. To say, even silently to myself, that David was dead. As if naming the loss might make it final, irreversible. As long as I kept searching, some small, irrational part of me could pretend there was still hope.

The widow who owned the house where I rented my attic room had grown frailer as winter progressed. Her cataract-clouded eyes saw less and less, and I had taken to helping her with small tasks—bringing in coal for her small stove, reading aloud the increasingly restrictive German proclamations posted throughout the city, occasionally sharing what meagre food I could procure. In return, she asked no questions about my comings and goings, about the absence of a yellow star on my coat, about the nightmares that sometimes woke me crying out in the darkness.

"You remind me of my son," she told me one evening as I built up her fire. "He had the same way of moving. Quiet, like a shadow."

Her son had died in the Great War, I knew. One of thousands of Dutch casualties despite the country's neutrality. His photograph stood on her mantel, a young man in uniform, smiling with the innocent confidence of someone who doesn't yet know his own mortality.

"Where is your family?" she asked, not for the first time. Her memory had begun to slip, questions and stories repeating in an endless loop.

"Zeeland," I answered, the same answer I always gave. "Near the coast."

She nodded, satisfied. "You should visit them. Family is everything in times like these."

I made a noncommittal sound, unwilling to explain the impossibility of such a journey, the permits required, the checkpoints to be navigated, the fear of my false papers being examined too closely. The letters I had sent remained unanswered—whether because they never arrived or because there was no one left to answer, I couldn't know.

"Soon," I said, to comfort her. "When the weather improves."

That night, I dreamed of David again. Not the nightmare of searching, of calling his name in a landscape of ruins. This was different. We were in the bakery, in the time before. David was kneading dough, his hands strong and sure, flour dusting his forearms. He was laughing at something I had said, his head thrown back, throat exposed, vulnerable and beautiful. The sunlight caught in his hair, turning the dark curls almost auburn. He looked at me, his amber eyes bright with amusement and something deeper, something just for me.

"You worry too much," he said, reaching out to brush flour from my cheek. "Everything will be alright."

I woke with tears on my face and his name on my lips.

Outside, the wind howled around the eaves of the old house, driving snow against the small window. The temperature in the attic had dropped well below freezing, my breath visible in the dim light of early morning. I wrapped my blanket more tightly around myself, reluctant to leave even the illusion of warmth it provided.

Eventually, necessity drove me from the bed. I dressed quickly, adding layers against the cold—a second shirt beneath my sweater, an extra pair of socks, the scarf I had found abandoned in a bombed building. The routine was familiar now: check that my false papers were secure in my inner pocket, ensure no trace of my Jewish identity was visible, prepare my mind for another day of vigilance and caution.

The widow was not yet awake when I descended the narrow stairs. I added coal to her stove, arranged kindling for when she would light it later, and slipped out into the bitter cold of a Rotterdam morning.

The streets were eerily quiet. New snow had fallen overnight, softening the sounds of the few people brave enough to venture out before dawn. I pulled my cap lower, tucked my hands into my pockets, and began the walk to the docks where I had found occasional work. The cold air burned in my lungs, but the physical discomfort was almost welcome—a distraction from the lingering sadness of the dream, from the constant weight of fear and loss.

I had nearly reached the harbour when I noticed something unusual. A German truck was parked at an intersection ahead, soldiers gathered around it, their breath fogging in the frigid air. More concerning was the small group of civilians already loaded in the back, huddled together against the cold. Even from a distance, I could see the yellow stars on their coats.

A raid. The Germans had been conducting them sporadically throughout the fall—surrounding a block or neighbourhood, checking papers, arresting those found with irregularities or attempting to hide their Jewish identity. But this was the first I had encountered directly.

I slowed my pace, assessing options. To turn back would draw attention, mark me as suspicious. To continue forward meant facing inspection, risking discovery of my false papers. Neither choice offered safety.

Before I could decide, more trucks appeared, blocking the street behind me. Soldiers jumped down, rifles ready, and began moving systematically through the nearby buildings. I was caught between, with nowhere to go but forward.

Heart pounding, I continued walking, trying to project the casual confidence of someone with nothing to hide. My papers were good—Joseph's associate had done his work well. But they weren't perfect. A thorough examination might reveal discrepancies. And there was always the possibility that my name was on some list, as Fritz Neumann had suggested by the river.

As I approached the checkpoint, I kept my gaze down, shoulders hunched against the cold. A line had formed as soldiers checked papers, separating those with yellow stars from those without, directing some to the waiting trucks, allowing others to continue.

I joined the queue, fighting to keep my breathing steady, my face impassive. Ahead of me, an elderly man fumbled with his identity card, his hands shaking either from cold or fear. The soldier examining it barked something in German, impatient. Then, with a sharp gesture, directed the old man toward the trucks.

My turn came. I presented my papers to a young soldier whose face was reddened by the cold. He glanced at them, then at me, comparing the photograph to my face. I kept my expression neutral, fighting the urge to fidget or look away.

"Occupation?" he asked in heavily accented Dutch.

"Baker," I answered, the word catching in my dry throat.

He looked down at my papers again, frowning slightly. My heart skipped. Had he noticed something? Some flaw in the documentation? Some sign that marked me as what I truly was?

Then, from behind him, another voice. "Is there a problem?"

I looked up to find myself staring into familiar pale eyes. Fritz Neumann, the German lieutenant from the river. He stood slightly apart from the other soldiers, his uniform impeccable despite the early hour and harsh weather.

The young soldier straightened. "No, sir. Just checking his papers."

Fritz's gaze met mine, betraying no recognition. "And? Are they in order?"

"Yes, sir. He can pass."

Fritz nodded once, dismissing both the soldier and me with the gesture. I tucked my papers back into my pocket and moved forward, legs weak with relief. I had nearly reached the end of the block when a voice stopped me.

"You. Wait."

I turned slowly to find Fritz approaching, his expression unreadable. The other soldiers continued their work, paying us no attention.

"Follow me," he said quietly. "Don't run."

Every instinct screamed to flee, but I knew it would be futile. Running would only confirm guilt, provide excuse for whatever was to come. So I followed as he led me away from the checkpoint, down a narrow side street partially blocked by snowdrifts.

When we were out of sight of the other soldiers, he stopped and turned to face me. "You need to leave this area. Now."

I stared at him, confused. "What?"

"They have your name," he said, his voice low and urgent. "The real one. Someone informed. They know your papers are false."

Cold fear washed through me, more bitter than the winter air. "How do you—"

"There isn't time," he cut me off. "This raid is just the beginning. They're moving through the entire district, building by building. If they find you..." He didn't finish the sentence. He didn't need to.

I struggled to make sense of what was happening. This German officer, this representative of the force that had destroyed Rotterdam, that had taken David from me, was warning me. Trying to help me. Nothing made sense.

"Why?" I managed.

Fritz glanced over his shoulder, checking that we were still alone. "Because..." He hesitated, something vulnerable flickering across his face. "Because sometimes we must do what we can. Even when it's not enough."

Before I could respond, he pressed something into my hand. A piece of paper, folded small. "Go to this address. Tonight. After curfew." His eyes held mine, intense, almost pleading. "If you want to live, Arthijs van Leeuwen, be there."

Then he was gone, striding back toward the checkpoint, leaving me holding the paper and a confusion of emotions I couldn't begin to untangle.

I waited until I was several blocks away before looking at what he had given me. An address, scrawled in precise handwriting. A location near the old harbour, not far from where the bakery had once stood.

The rest of the day passed in a fog of fear and uncertainty. I avoided returning to my attic room, aware now that it might no longer be safe. Instead, I wandered the less patrolled areas of the city, trying to think, to plan, to understand what was happening and what I should do.

Fritz Neumann knew my real identity. He knew my papers were false. He appeared to be trying to help me—but why? What possible reason could a German officer have for warning a Jew about raids, for providing a potential escape? It could be a trap, a way to lure those in hiding into revealing themselves. But that made little sense when he could have simply arrested me at the checkpoint.

As darkness fell and curfew approached, I found myself drawn toward the address he had given me. Curiosity, desperation, and the simple lack of alternatives propelled me through streets growing empty as people hurried to the safety of their homes before the curfew bells rang.

The location was a warehouse, seemingly abandoned like many along this stretch of the harbour. The bombing had damaged most of the structures here, and few had been repaired or reclaimed. In the gathering darkness, with snow beginning to fall again, the building loomed like a ghost of Rotterdam's former prosperity.

I hesitated at a distance, watching for movement, for any sign that this was indeed a trap. Nothing. Just the soft hiss of snow falling on stone, the distant groan of damaged buildings settling in the cold. After nearly an hour of surveillance, with curfew now fully in effect, I approached.

The main doors were chained shut, but a smaller door to the side was unlocked. I slipped inside, immediately enveloped in darkness and the musty scent of long-abandoned space. My eyes adjusted slowly, revealing the cavernous interior—empty except for a few broken crates and the skeletal remains of machinery.

"You came."

The voice startled me. I spun to find Fritz emerging from the shadows near what might once have been an office. He was alone, and—most surprisingly—out of uniform. He wore civilian clothes, dark and nondescript, with a cap pulled low over his fair hair.

"What is this?" I demanded, keeping my distance. "Why am I here?"

Fritz regarded me steadily. "Because by morning, your room will be raided. Your landlady will be questioned. And you will be arrested, if you're there to be found."

A chill ran through me that had nothing to do with the frigid air. "How do you know this?"

"I have access to the lists. The schedules." He took a tentative step forward. "I saw your name. Again."

I remembered our first meeting by the river, his mention of seeing my name on a list. "Why would you warn me? You're one of them."

A shadow crossed his face. "Yes. I wear their uniform. I follow most of their orders." His gaze dropped briefly. "But there are lines I cannot cross. Even now."

None of this made sense. A German officer with apparent scruples about the persecution of Jews? It had to be a ruse, a complex trap. Yet instinct told me otherwise. The same instinct that had recognised something in him that day by the river—something that didn't belong in that uniform any more than I belonged in a city where my people were being hunted.

"What do you want from me?" I asked, the question emerging more vulnerable than I had intended.

Fritz reached inside his coat and withdrew a bundle. When he held it out, I recognised it immediately—a German uniform, folded neatly.

"Put this on," he said quietly. "It's the only way we'll get through the checkpoints."

I stared at the uniform, the embodiment of everything I had come to hate and fear. "You want me to wear... that?"

"I want you to survive," Fritz replied, his voice steady. "This is how."

I made no move to take it. "And go where? Where could possibly be safe now?"

"I have a place," he said, a hint of impatience entering his tone. "But we must go now, before the night patrols change. Each moment we delay increases the risk."

The entire situation felt surreal, dreamlike. A German officer offering escape. The enemy's uniform as protection. A place of safety, when nowhere in Rotterdam—perhaps nowhere in Europe—was truly safe for someone like me.

Yet what choice did I have? Return to my room, wait for the raid that Fritz promised would come? Try to flee the city alone, in winter, without papers that would allow me past checkpoints? Or trust this stranger who had already spared me once, who seemed to be risking his own safety to help me?

"Why?" I asked again, needing to understand before I could decide. "Why would you do this?"

Fritz was silent for a long moment, his expression unreadable in the dim light. Then, quietly, "Because I've seen what happens to those who are taken. Where they go. What awaits them." He swallowed visibly. "And because when I saw you by the river that day, I recognised something familiar. Something I see in my own mirror each morning."

The implication hung in the air between us, unspoken but clear. This German soldier, this enemy, was suggesting a commonality I had refused to acknowledge even to myself. That beyond our obvious differences—Jew and German, occupied and occupier—lay a deeper shared identity. A secret that could destroy us both.

I took the uniform, the weight of it heavy in my arms. Heavy with meaning, with choice, with consequence.

"Change quickly," Fritz said, turning away to give me privacy. "We don't have much time."

I did as he directed, shedding my civilian clothes for the hated uniform. It fit poorly, too long in the limbs, too loose across the shoulders. But in the darkness, with the cap pulled low, the disguise might work. Might allow me to walk past those who would otherwise arrest me on sight.

When I had finished, Fritz approached and made small adjustments, correcting the angle of the cap, straightening insignia I didn't recognise or understand. His fingers worked efficiently, impersonally, yet I was intensely aware of each touch, each moment of contact.

"Remember," he said, stepping back to inspect his work, "walk with purpose. Look directly ahead. Speak as little as possible, and let me do any talking that's necessary." He switched to German, adding, "Verstanden?"

I nodded, not trusting myself to attempt the language of my enemies.

"Good." Fritz moved toward the side door, pausing to check the street before gesturing for me to follow. "Stay close. Do exactly as I do."

We stepped out into the snowy night, two German soldiers on some official business, moving with the confidence of those who owned the city. I mimicked Fritz's posture, his gait, fighting the urge to hunch my shoulders or look down as I normally would. Every step felt like a betrayal, yet also a bizarre liberation—for the first time in months, I walked without fear of being stopped, questioned, discovered.

The streets were largely empty, curfew having driven most indoors. The few German patrols we passed paid us little attention—a brief nod of acknowledgment, perhaps, but no challenges, no requests for identification or explanation. The uniform worked its dark magic, rendering me invisible in plain sight.

Fritz led us on a winding route, avoiding the most heavily patrolled areas, keeping to streets where shadows provided additional cover. We passed buildings where I had once felt at home, corners where David and I had paused to share a private glance or brush of hands, shops where we had bought bread or coffee in what now seemed like another lifetime.

Rotterdam by night, in winter, under occupation, was a city of ghosts. And I was one of them, moving unseen through streets that had once known me.

At one point, we had to cross a major intersection where a checkpoint had been established. My heart raced as we approached, the uniform suddenly feeling like the flimsiest of disguises. Fritz must have sensed my tension.

"Steady," he murmured. "Remember who you're pretending to be."

The soldiers at the checkpoint straightened as we approached. One stepped forward, hand raised in a casual salute. He said something in German, too quick for me to catch. Fritz responded in the same language, his tone confident, slightly bored, as if this interaction was routine and beneath his notice.

The soldier nodded and stepped aside, allowing us to pass. I kept my face impassive, gaze forward, breathing only when we were safely beyond their view.

"What did he say?" I asked when we had turned onto a quieter street.

"He asked if we'd heard about the raid scheduled for tomorrow," Fritz replied, his voice grim. "I said yes, we were just discussing it."

The casual confirmation of what awaited at my former lodgings sent a chill through me. Had I not met Fritz, had I returned to the widow's house tonight, I would have been taken in that raid. Loaded onto a truck like those I had seen this morning. Sent to whatever fate Fritz had alluded to, the fate he had seen and could not speak of directly.

I owed him my freedom, perhaps my life. The realization was uncomfortable, complex. How could I be indebted to someone who served the regime that had destroyed everything I loved? Yet here we were, walking side by side through the snow, connected by secrets neither of us had fully acknowledged.

After nearly an hour of tense progress through the occupied city, Fritz led us to a modest house on a quiet street near the harbour. Nothing distinguished it from its neighbours—the same narrow construction, the same partially repaired bomb damage, the same darkened windows observing curfew.

Fritz checked the street once more, then quickly unlocked the door and ushered me inside. Only when the door was closed and locked behind us did he relax slightly, removing his cap and gesturing for me to do the same.

The house was cold and dark, but as my eyes adjusted, I could make out simple furnishings, a setting of austere functionality rather than comfort. Fritz moved with the familiarity of someone at home, lighting a small lamp that cast soft shadows across walls bare of any personal touches.

"You live here?" I asked, suddenly uncertain again. I had imagined being taken to some safe house, some hidden space where others like me might be sheltered. Not to a German officer's private residence.

Fritz nodded, setting the lamp on a table. "It's safe. No one will look for you here." A ghost of a smile touched his lips, bitter and brief. "The last place they would expect to find a Jew is in the home of a Wehrmacht lieutenant."

The truth of this was undeniable, yet it offered little comfort. I stood awkwardly in the small front room, still wearing the hated uniform, suddenly acutely aware of my vulnerability. I was alone with a virtual stranger, a German soldier, in a house no one knew I had entered. If this was indeed a trap, it was one from which there would be no escape.

Fritz seemed to read my thoughts. "You're safe here," he repeated, his voice softening. "I give you my word."

"The word of a German officer?" I couldn't keep the bitterness from my voice.

He flinched slightly but didn't argue. "Yes. For whatever that's worth to you." He moved to a small stove in the corner and began preparing to light it. "You should change. There are clothes upstairs that might fit you. First door on the right."

I hesitated, torn between the desire to be free of the uniform and reluctance to move deeper into this unfamiliar space, to make myself at home in the enemy's house.

Fritz looked up from his task, something like understanding in his pale eyes. "I know this is... difficult. Impossible, perhaps. To trust me. To be here." He straightened, his gaze direct. "But I am trying to help you, Arthijs. Whatever you believe about me, believe that."

The use of my name, spoken quietly in his accented Dutch, broke something in me. The fear, the confusion, the bone-deep exhaustion of months spent surviving—it all crashed over me like a wave. I sank onto a nearby chair, suddenly unable to stand.

"Why?" I asked yet again, the question that wouldn't leave me. "Why me? Why risk everything for a stranger?"

Fritz was silent for a long moment, his attention seemingly focused on getting the stove lit. The small flame that finally caught illuminated his profile—the straight nose, the firm jaw, the troubled brow. He was younger than I had initially thought, probably no older than I was, though responsibility and war had aged him prematurely.

"Because you're not a stranger," he said finally, still not looking at me. "Not really." He added wood to the small flame, careful, methodical. "That day by the river... I saw something in you. Something I recognised." He glanced up briefly. "Something dangerous for both of us."

The implication hung in the air between us, neither of us willing to name it directly. The shared secret that could destroy us both—him as much as me, perhaps more so, given his position.

"So this is... what? Sympathy from one outsider to another?" I asked, wariness battling with a growing, unwilling understanding.

Fritz shook his head. "Not sympathy. Recognition." He closed the stove door, the small fire now catching properly. "And perhaps a selfish desire to do one right thing in the midst of so much wrong. To save one life when so many are being taken."

The rawness in his voice, the genuine anguish, was impossible to dismiss as mere pretence. This man, this German officer in his immaculate uniform, was indeed trying to help me. For reasons complex and perhaps not fully understood even by himself, but genuine nonetheless.

"The clothes," he said, changing the subject abruptly. "Go change. We can talk more once you're comfortable. Once you're warm."

I stood, still uncertain but no longer paralyzed by fear. Whatever Fritz Neumann's intentions, whatever lay ahead, I had survived this night. Had escaped the raid that would have taken me. Was, for the moment at least, safe.

As I climbed the narrow stairs to find the promised civilian clothes, I felt something shifting within me—a cautious, tentative trust beginning to form. Not complete, not unquestioning, but present. A fragile bridge across the chasm that separated us.

Behind me, I heard Fritz moving in the small kitchen, preparing what might be tea or soup. The domestic normalcy of it was surreal after the tension of our flight through occupied Rotterdam. Yet it was also oddly comforting—a reminder that even in the midst of war and hatred, small human kindnesses remained possible.

I reached the top of the stairs and paused, looking back down at the German soldier who had risked everything to save a Jewish stranger. Who had recognised in me something he saw in himself. Who had, against all odds and expectations, become my unlikely protector.

Fritz looked up, catching my gaze. For a moment, neither of us spoke. Then he nodded once, a silent acknowledgment of the unspoken understanding growing between us.

I continued to the bedroom, to the promised change of clothes. To the next uncertain chapter of a life that had become a series of losses and unexpected turns.

To whatever safety this enemy's house might offer in a world where safety had become as rare as hope.

CHAPTER 9: THE CUPBOARD

Rotterdam, 1941

The first day in the cupboard was the longest of my life.

After that night of escape through the snowy streets of Rotterdam—Fritz leading me past German checkpoints in a borrowed uniform—I had expected to remain hidden in his house. It seemed the logical sanctuary, as he had said himself: who would look for a Jew in a German officer's home? But Fritz had other plans.

"It's not safe," he explained the next morning, his voice low though we were alone in the small kitchen. "My superior officers visit sometimes. Unannounced. And neighbours watch. They notice patterns, visitors."

I stared into the weak tea he had prepared, the liquid barely darker than water, a reflection of wartime shortages that affected even those who served the Reich. "Then where?"

Fritz hesitated, choosing his words carefully. "There's a warehouse. Near the old harbour. Used for storage sometimes, but mostly forgotten since the bombing." He glanced up, meeting my eyes directly. "There's a large cupboard there. Former office storage. Hidden behind stacked crates. No one would think to look."

"A cupboard," I repeated, the word flat in my mouth.

He nodded, his expression grim but determined. "It's temporary. Until I can arrange something better."

I wanted to protest, to argue that surely there were safer options, resistance networks, people who specialised in hiding Jews. But the truth was, I had nowhere else to go. No connections to underground movements, no friends still free who might help. Fritz Neumann, this German officer with his conflicted pale eyes and unexpected mercy, was my only hope.

"How long?" I asked.

"I don't know," he admitted. "A few weeks, perhaps. No longer than necessary."

It would be three months.

The cupboard was exactly as Fritz had described—a tall wooden storage cabinet in the back corner of an abandoned warehouse, hidden from casual view by stacked shipping crates. It smelled of dust and old paper, with just enough space for a man to sit with knees drawn up or to lie curled on his side. Fritz had prepared it as best he could, lining the bottom with blankets, leaving a small lantern, matches, a bucket for necessary functions, and as much food and water as could be safely stored.

"I'll come when I can," he promised as he prepared to leave me there that first day. "Every few days, at least. To bring food, empty the bucket." He handed me a small knife. "If anyone discovers you..."

I took it, understanding what he couldn't quite say. A last resort, should the worst happen. Though whether it was meant for potential captors or myself remained unsaid.

"Thank you," I told him, the words inadequate for what he was risking.

Fritz's expression softened briefly. "Bleib sicher," he said. Stay safe. Then he closed the cupboard door, and I was alone in the darkness.

The first few hours weren't so bad. The space, while confining, wasn't unbearable. I could stretch one leg at a time, could sit upright if I hunched my shoulders, could even turn from one side to the other with careful manoeuvring. The darkness was almost complete, but the small lantern provided brief comfort when needed, though I rationed its use carefully, aware that the oil might need to last weeks.

I had survived worse, I told myself. The bombing. The months of searching for David. The constant fear of discovery. This was just another trial to endure, another passage to navigate on the long journey toward whatever waited at the end—survival or reunion or simply a more dignified end than being taken in a German raid.

But as the hours stretched into days, the reality of my confinement began to weigh on me. The physical discomfort was considerable—muscles cramping from lack of movement, joints stiffening, skin growing tender where bones pressed against the hard wood. But worse was the psychological toll. The silence, broken only by distant harbour sounds or the occasional shuffle of rats in the warehouse beyond my wooden prison. The darkness, which seemed to grow thicker rather than more navigable as time passed. The crushing awareness of how little separated me from discovery—just a wooden door, a few stacked crates, the fragile protection of a German officer whose motives I still didn't fully understand.

I tried to create routines to maintain my sanity. I divided each day into segments marked by small rituals. Morning began with gentle stretches, as much as the confined space allowed. Midday brought a small portion of whatever food Fritz had left. Evening included quietly recited prayers, words from my childhood that brought comfort even as I questioned whether anyone was listening. Night was the hardest—thoughts of David, of Noah, of all I had lost cascading through my mind as I tried to find sleep in my cramped nest of blankets.

I kept track of days by marking the inside of the cupboard with the knife Fritz had given me. Small, discreet notches that wouldn't be visible to anyone opening the door, but allowed me to maintain some tenuous connection to time's passage. Without them, I might have slipped into believing I had been there for years rather than days, or conversely, that only hours had passed when it had been a week.

Fritz came as promised, though not on any schedule I could discern. Sometimes three days would pass between visits, sometimes five. He always came at night, when the risk of being seen was lowest. The sound of the warehouse door opening would send my heart racing—was it Fritz, or discovery? I would press my ear to the cupboard door, listening for his familiar tread, the quiet code-knock he used to signal it was safe to emerge briefly.

Those moments outside the cupboard became my lifeline. Standing upright, stretching fully, breathing air that wasn't stale with my own exhalations—these simple pleasures became profound luxuries. Fritz would bring fresh water, food wrapped carefully in paper, occasionally even luxuries like soap or a book.

"It's not much," he would apologise, as if the risk he took bringing these items was insignificant.

"It's everything," I would answer, meaning it.

Our early interactions were cautious, practical, focused on immediate needs. He would empty the bucket I used for waste, replace my water jug, hand over food that I would consume slowly, savouring each bite. We spoke little at first, the gulf between our circumstances too vast for casual conversation.

But as weeks passed, something shifted. Perhaps it was the intimacy forced upon us by the situation—Fritz seeing to my most basic needs, myself utterly dependent on his mercy. Perhaps it was the shared risk, the knowledge that discovery would mean death for us both. Or perhaps it was simply the human need for connection asserting itself even in the most dire circumstances.

We began to talk during his visits. Brief exchanges at first, then longer conversations as I was permitted to sit outside the cupboard, stretching my legs while he kept watch near the warehouse door.

"How did you become an officer?" I asked one night in late January, almost a month into my confinement. "You seem... different from the others."

Fritz's smile was bitter in the dim light of the lantern he had brought. "I was a university student. Engineering. When war seemed inevitable, I volunteered, thinking it better than being drafted." He shook his head slightly. "A foolish calculation. But I tested well, showed aptitude for languages and mathematics. They sent me to officer training instead of the front."

"And now you're here. In Rotterdam."

"Yes. Assigned to the occupation administration." His voice grew quieter. "I thought it would be better than combat. Less... direct participation." His gaze dropped to his hands. "I was wrong about that too."

I studied him in the soft light—his fair hair cropped short in military fashion, his face younger than his bearing suggested, the uniform that marked him as my enemy worn with a discomfort I was beginning to recognise.

"Why are you helping me?" I asked again, the question that never quite left me despite the growing evidence of his sincerity.

Fritz was silent for a long moment. "Because I can," he finally said. "Because it's the only thing I can do that doesn't..." He struggled for words. "That doesn't soil me further." He looked up, his pale eyes haunted. "And because when I saw you that day by the river, I recognised something of myself. Something I've hidden all my life."

The unspoken truth hung between us, acknowledged yet unnamed. This shared secret that placed us both outside society's acceptance, that made us both vulnerable in different but parallel ways.

"How did you know?" I asked, my voice barely audible. "About me?"

"I didn't. Not with certainty." His gaze was steady. "But I saw how you looked at me. Not with the hatred I usually see from the Dutch, not with the fear I see from Jews. With... recognition." A small, sad smile touched his lips. "We learn to see our own kind, don't we? Even when we wish we couldn't."

I nodded, unable to deny it. David and I had developed that same awareness—the ability to recognise others like us, to communicate through glances and small gestures while keeping our true selves hidden from the world.

"There was someone," I said, the words emerging before I'd fully decided to speak them. "Before the bombing. His name was David."

Fritz waited, not pressing, allowing me the space to continue or retreat as I chose.

"He worked with me at the bakery. He was..." I swallowed against the sudden tightness in my throat. "He was everything. And then the bombs came."

"I'm sorry," Fritz said softly. And I believed him—believed that this German officer truly regretted the destruction his country had rained upon mine, the loss of the man I had loved.

"Have you ever..." I began, then hesitated, unsure how to ask what I wanted to know.

"Had someone?" Fritz finished for me. He shook his head. "No. Not in any real way. There have been... encounters. Brief, anonymous. Nothing lasting." His expression grew distant. "In our world, in uniform especially, it's too dangerous."

I thought of the risk he was taking hiding me—not just as a Jew, but as someone who represented a part of himself he had never been permitted to acknowledge openly. The courage it required seemed suddenly staggering.

"Thank you," I said, the words encompassing more than gratitude for food or water or temporary freedom from the cupboard.

Fritz understood. He nodded once, then glanced at his watch. "It's time. You need to go back in."

The return to confinement was always the hardest part of his visits. The cupboard, tolerable before seeing the open space of the warehouse, became a torture chamber afterward. But I crawled back in without complaint, knowing each minute Fritz remained increased his danger.

"I'll come again in three days," he promised, passing me a small package. "Here. Something to make the time pass."

Inside was a book—Goethe's poetry, in German. I looked up, questioning.

"I thought..." Fritz hesitated. "I thought perhaps you might want to practice the language. For..." He didn't finish, but I understood. For whatever came next. For the possibility of escape to somewhere German might be useful. For a future he was trying to help me reach.

"Thank you," I said again, clutching the small volume. "I'll study it carefully."

He nodded, his expression a complex mix of emotions I couldn't fully decipher. Then he closed the cupboard door, and I was alone again in my wooden prison.

The book became my most precious possession. By the wan light of the lantern, I traced the German words, translating what I could, guessing at what I couldn't. The language of my enemies became a rope pulling me toward sanity, each new word mastered a small victory against the darkness pressing in around me.

February brought deeper cold that penetrated the warehouse walls and made my cupboard a frigid cell. The blankets Fritz had provided were insufficient against the bitter chill that seemed to seep into my bones. I developed a constant cough, my lungs irritated by the dust and the damp. Sleep became even more elusive, my body shivering too violently for rest.

Fritz arrived one night to find me huddled in a corner of the cupboard, teeth chattering uncontrollably. Without a word, he helped me out, wrapped his own coat around my shoulders, and sat beside me until warmth began to return to my limbs.

"This can't continue," he said, his voice tight with concern. "You'll die in there."

"What choice do we have?" I asked, the words punctuated by coughs.

He was silent for a moment, consideration in his pale eyes. "I might have another option. My house has an attic. Small, rarely used. If we were careful..."

Hope flared briefly, then dimmed as I considered the risks. "Your neighbours. Your superior officers. You said yourself it was too dangerous."

"This is more dangerous," Fritz insisted, gesturing toward my shivering form. "Pneumonia will kill you as surely as discovery, and more painfully." He shook his head. "We'll be careful. I'll prepare a hiding place within the attic, for when others visit. It can work."

I wanted to believe him. Wanted desperately to escape the cupboard that had become both sanctuary and torment. But the thought of placing Fritz in even greater danger gave me pause.

"Why would you risk more for me?" I asked, needing to understand before I could accept.

Fritz was quiet for a long time, his gaze on the warehouse floor. When he finally looked up, there was a rawness in his expression I hadn't seen before.

"Because in helping you, I help myself," he said softly. "Because each time I bring you food, or books, or moments of freedom from that box, I reclaim some small part of the person I was before this uniform." His hand made a small, dismissive gesture toward his immaculate Wehrmacht attire. "Because you're the only person who sees me—really sees me."

The honesty in his voice was unmistakable. This wasn't mere sympathy or abstract moral principle. This was something more personal, more profound. Fritz Neumann was trying to save us both—me from physical destruction, himself from moral annihilation.

"When?" I asked, accepting his offer because there was no real alternative, because the cupboard would indeed kill me eventually, because the connection growing between us demanded acknowledgment.

"Two days," he said, relief evident in his voice. "I need time to prepare the attic, to create a schedule for ensuring your safety." He hesitated. "It won't be freedom. You'll still be confined, hidden. But it will be better than this."

"Anything would be," I admitted, another bout of coughing punctuating the truth of my words.

Fritz nodded, then surprised me by reaching out to briefly clasp my shoulder. The touch was tentative, almost awkward, yet conveyed a compassion I had thought lost in Rotterdam's ruins.

"Two more days," he promised. "Then we'll get you out of here."

As he helped me back into the cupboard for what we both hoped would be the final time, I felt something shift between us. The German officer and the hidden Jew. The enemy and the fugitive. The man hiding his true nature behind a uniform and the man hiding his entire existence in a wooden box. Somehow, improbably, we had become something neither of us had words for yet.

Not quite friends. Not quite allies. Something more complex, something forged in the crucible of war and shared danger and mutual recognition.

Something, I realised as the cupboard door closed once more, that might sustain us both through whatever darkness still lay ahead.

CHAPTER 10: THE ATTIC

Rotterdam, 1941-1942

The first taste of real warmth was overwhelming.

After three months in the warehouse cupboard, the heat from Fritz's small stove hit me like a physical force as we entered his house. It was early March 1941, and the winter's grip on Rotterdam remained fierce. The journey had been perilous—me disguised once again in a German uniform, Fritz leading the way through streets emptied by curfew and bitter cold.

"Quickly," Fritz murmured, securing the door behind us. "Upstairs."

I followed him through the sparsely furnished house, still light-headed from the combination of illness and sudden warmth. My lungs burned with each breath, the cough I'd developed in the cupboard having settled deep in my chest. Three months of confinement had weakened me more than I wanted to admit.

The stairs creaked slightly under our weight as we climbed to the second floor, then Fritz reached up to pull down a ladder that led to the attic. He gestured for me to ascend first, steadying the wooden rungs as I climbed awkwardly, my stiff limbs protesting every movement.

The attic was small, with a sharply slanted ceiling that allowed standing room only in the centre. A single dormer window, blacked out with heavy fabric, suggested where daylight might enter if permitted. The space was clean but austere—a narrow mattress on the floor, a small table with a lamp, a chamber pot discreetly placed in one corner. Fritz had clearly prepared it with care, though with an eye toward utility rather than comfort.

"It's not much," he said, echoing the apology he'd offered so many times about provisions brought to the cupboard.

"It's a palace," I replied, meaning it entirely. After the cupboard, this modest attic truly seemed luxurious—space to stand upright, to lie flat while sleeping, to move more than a few inches in any direction.

Fritz nodded, understanding. "There's food in that box," he said, pointing to a small wooden crate near the mattress. "Water in the pitcher. Books under the bed." He hesitated. "And this."

From inside his coat, he withdrew a small radio, its case scratched and worn but intact.

"It only receives local broadcasts," he explained, setting it carefully on the table. "German-controlled, of course. But it's something. A connection to the outside world."

I stared at the radio, recognizing the risk it represented. Discovery would be bad enough; discovery with a radio—a potential link to resistance communications—would be catastrophic.

"Thank you," I said, overwhelmed by the gesture.

Fritz's expression softened briefly. "There's one more thing to show you." He moved to what appeared to be a solid wall near the chimney stack that ran up through the attic. "If anyone comes—if you hear voices below or footsteps on the stairs—you hide here."

His fingers found a nearly invisible seam in the wooden panelling. With practiced movements, he slid a section aside, revealing a narrow space between the attic wall and the chimney—a gap barely wide enough for a man to stand in, completely hidden when the panel was closed.

"I built it myself," Fritz said, a hint of pride in his voice. "Even if they search the attic, they won't find this. Not unless they know to look for it specifically."

I examined the hiding place, impressed by its construction despite the claustrophobia that threatened at the thought of being confined in such a tight space. After the cupboard, I had hoped never to be enclosed again. But this was different—this was safety, not imprisonment. A last resort, not a permanent condition.

"Thank you," I said again, the words woefully inadequate for what Fritz had done—was doing—for me.

He nodded once, acknowledging more than my spoken gratitude. "I need to go back out. Establish that I was on patrol, create witnesses who saw me elsewhere tonight." He gestured toward the mattress. "Rest. Your cough won't improve without proper sleep."

I wanted to protest, to insist I was stronger than I appeared, but exhaustion was already pulling at me, making the simple mattress seem irresistibly inviting.

"I'll return in the morning before my shift," Fritz continued. "No one will visit tonight." He paused at the ladder. "You're safe here, Arthijs."

Then he was gone, descending with quiet efficiency, leaving me alone in my new sanctuary.

I sank onto the mattress, my body grateful for a softness it had nearly forgotten. The attic was cool but not cold, the house's heat rising sufficiently to take the dangerous chill from the air. I wrapped myself in the blankets Fritz had provided, their weight a comfort after months of inadequate covering.

Sleep came almost instantly, pulling me under before I could even fully process the strangeness of my new situation—hidden in the attic of a German officer's house, dependent on the enemy for my very survival, yet feeling safer than I had since the bombing that had taken everything from me.

I woke to soft grey light filtering through a small gap in the window covering and the distant sounds of Rotterdam beginning its day under occupation—the rumble of military vehicles, the calls of vendors selling what meagre goods remained available, the church bells that still rang despite everything.

For a disorienting moment, I couldn't remember where I was. The absence of the cupboard's confining walls, the unfamiliar feel of the mattress beneath me, the relative warmth—all seemed like elements of a dream from which I would soon wake to find myself back in my wooden prison.

Then memory returned, bringing with it a surge of gratitude so intense it was almost painful. I was in Fritz's attic. I could stand up. I could stretch my arms outward. I could breathe air that wasn't stale with dust and my own exhalations.

I rose carefully, my body still weak from illness and confinement but already responding to the improved conditions. The cough remained, but seemed less fierce than the day before. I explored my new space more thoroughly in the dim light—noting the careful details of Fritz's preparations.

The food box contained bread, dried fruit, a precious small tin of meat preserves. The books stacked beneath the bed ranged from simple German grammar texts to novels in both Dutch and German. There was even a notebook and pencil, luxuries I hadn't expected.

Most surprising was a small basin with soap and a towel, suggesting the possibility of washing—something that had been largely impossible in the cupboard. I used some of the water from the pitcher to wet the towel, then cleaned myself as best I could, the simple act feeling almost ceremonial after months of accumulated grime.

As I finished this makeshift ablution, I heard the front door open below. Instinctively, I froze, listening intently. Then came Fritz's distinctive tread on the stairs, and I relaxed, settling back onto the mattress as the attic ladder descended.

Fritz appeared moments later, carrying a small covered pot that released tantalizing aromas as he climbed into the attic.

"Porridge," he explained, setting it before me. "Not much, but warm. And there's real coffee."

My stomach clenched at the mention of hot food, something I hadn't experienced since before the cupboard. Words failed me as Fritz uncovered the pot to reveal the simple porridge, steam rising invitingly from its surface.

He watched me eat, satisfaction evident in his expression. "Your cough sounds better," he observed. "The warmth is helping."

I nodded, unwilling to speak until I had savoured every spoonful of the simple meal. Only when the pot was empty did I finally manage, "Thank you. For all of this."

Fritz waved away my gratitude. "You'll need to be especially careful today," he said, shifting to practical matters. "I have meetings at headquarters until evening. The house should remain empty, but if anyone comes, use the hiding place immediately. Don't wait to gather your things. Just move."

I nodded, sobered by the reminder of my precarious situation. The attic was an improvement beyond measure, but discovery would mean death—for me certainly, likely for Fritz as well.

"I understand," I assured him.

"Good." He collected the empty pot. "I've left a bucket of water by the ladder. For washing, if you wish. Just be careful not to spill it." He glanced around the attic once more, checking that everything was in order. "I'll return around eight."

Then he was gone again, descending to resume his role as Lieutenant Neumann, loyal officer of the occupying force, while I settled into my new existence as his secret burden.

The day passed with excruciating slowness. Despite the relative comforts of the attic, confinement remained confinement. I rationed my exploration of Fritz's provisions, examining each book before setting it aside, testing the radio's reception at the lowest possible volume, making small notes in the provided notebook—anything to occupy my mind.

The hidden radio proved both blessing and curse. The broadcasts were indeed German-controlled, full of propaganda about Reich victories and Allied defeats. But between the obvious lies were fragments of truth, hints about the war's progress that helped me understand the larger context of my small, hidden existence.

I learned that the Germans had invaded the Soviet Union in June 1941, opening an Eastern Front that stretched their forces. That American aid was flowing to Britain despite U.S. neutrality. That resistance movements were growing across occupied Europe.

None of this changed my immediate circumstances, but it provided perspective—a reminder that the world continued beyond the walls of my attic, that larger forces were in motion that might, eventually, lead to liberation.

As darkness fell, I grew increasingly anxious for Fritz's return. The house's settling noises, innocuous in daylight, became ominous in shadow. Each creak might herald an unexpected visitor; each distant voice on the street might belong to someone approaching the door.

When Fritz finally arrived, I felt a relief out of proportion to the hours of his absence. He brought more food—a thin vegetable soup and bread—and news from the outside world that the radio hadn't provided.

"They're increasing the restrictions on Jews," he said quietly as I ate. "More areas of the city forbidden. More businesses closed. More people being sent east."

East. We both knew what that meant, though neither of us spoke it aloud. The rumours had been circulating for months—camps somewhere in Poland where Jews were being sent. Labor camps, officially. But the stories that filtered back suggested something far worse.

"Thank you," I said, the words taking on new weight with each repetition. "For keeping me from that."

Fritz nodded, his expression troubled. "I should go. Early shift tomorrow."

And so began the pattern of our days—Fritz leaving for his duties each morning, returning briefly when possible, then again in the evening. Me, confined to the attic, establishing small rituals to maintain sanity in isolation. The arrangement was imperfect, fraught with danger for us both, yet infinitely preferable to the alternatives.

As March gave way to April, my health improved. The persistent cough finally faded, and strength returned to muscles weakened by cupboard confinement. The attic, initially a paradise compared to my previous prison, gradually revealed its own limitations—the inability to stand fully upright except in the centre, the need for constant quiet, the tedium of endless hours alone.

Fritz did what he could to alleviate these hardships. He brought books regularly, selecting titles he thought might interest me—history, philosophy, even poetry. He provided paper so I could write, though we agreed any pages I filled would need to be burned immediately for safety. He shared what news he could, filtering the propaganda to give me some sense of the war's true progress.

Most surprisingly, he began bringing items I hadn't requested, hadn't even mentioned wanting—small luxuries that seemed impossible in wartime Rotterdam. A piece of chocolate. A real egg. Once, incredibly, an orange, its bright colour almost shocking after months of visual deprivation.

When I asked how he obtained such things, Fritz was evasive. "Supply channels," he said vaguely. "It's better if you don't know details."

I suspected these items came at significant cost—either financial or in terms of risk—but Fritz dismissed my attempts to refuse them.

"Let me do this," he said simply. "It matters to me."

So I accepted, recognizing that these gifts served a purpose for him as well—small rebellions against the regime he outwardly served, tangible expressions of the humanity he struggled to maintain while wearing the uniform of oppression.

Our conversations, initially cautious and practical, gradually deepened. In the evenings, when Fritz could stay longer, we would talk—about our lives before the war, about books we had read, about philosophical questions that had no easy answers. We carefully avoided certain topics—David, whom I still couldn't discuss without pain; the actual operations Fritz participated in as part of the occupation forces; the likelihood of either of us surviving to see the war's end.

Instead, we built a fragile normalcy within our extraordinary circumstances. Fritz would bring news of the outside world—which shops had received deliveries, which streets had been newly restricted, which rumours were circulating among Rotterdam's citizens. I would share observations from my limited vantage point—changes in the patterns of air traffic overhead, variations in the church bells' ringing, shifts in the tone of radio broadcasts.

Most unexpected was the development of a ritual neither of us acknowledged directly. Each evening, before leaving, Fritz would place a hand briefly on my shoulder—a gesture that began as reassurance but evolved into something more, a physical confirmation of the connection growing between us despite everything that should have made it impossible.

I found myself looking forward to that moment each day—the simple human contact after hours of isolation, the warmth of another person's touch in a world gone cold with hatred and fear. It was nothing like what David and I had shared, nothing romantic or passionate, yet it sustained me in ways I couldn't fully articulate even to myself.

By summer, I had developed routines that helped mark the passage of time and maintain my sanity. Mornings began with simple exercises—stretches and movements modified to accommodate the attic's confines. Afternoons were for study—working through Fritz's German books, improving my comprehension of the language I still associated with enemies but now also with the man who had saved me. Evenings were for writing—poems, memories, reflections on my strange existence, all committed to paper and then consigned to flames before Fritz returned.

The radio became a lifeline, despite the propaganda it transmitted. I learned to listen between the words, to detect the subtle shifts in tone that suggested German setbacks even in broadcasts claiming victories. Fritz confirmed my interpretations when he could, adding details too sensitive for public announcement—growing resistance in occupied territories, increasing pressure on German supply lines, the toll of the Russian winter on Wehrmacht forces.

The war, it seemed, was not proceeding according to Hitler's plans. This knowledge provided a fragile hope—that perhaps, someday, this hiding might end. That Germany might be defeated. That surviving long enough might eventually mean freedom rather than just continued existence.

One particularly hot July evening, as we shared a simple meal of bread and cheese, Fritz surprised me with an unexpected question.

"Do you ever wonder about after?" he asked, his voice quiet in the attic's close air. "When this is over. What comes next."

I hesitated, uncertain how to respond. Thoughts of "after" seemed dangerous, tempting fate with premature hope. And yet, they were inevitable.

"Sometimes," I admitted. "But it's hard to imagine. The world has changed so completely."

Fritz nodded, his gaze distant. "I think about it often. Where I might go. What I might do." He looked at me directly. "Whether anything I do now can possibly balance what I've been part of."

The rawness in his voice caught me off guard. Fritz rarely spoke so openly about his internal conflicts, about the moral weight of his position within the occupation forces.

"You're saving a life," I said softly. "My life. That counts for something."

"One life against how many?" he countered, a bitterness in his tone I'd rarely heard. "The orders I relay. The actions I don't prevent. The system I serve, even reluctantly."

I had no easy answer for this. Fritz's guilt was justified—he was part of the machinery of occupation, of oppression, regardless of his personal misgivings or individual acts of rebellion. Yet I couldn't condemn the man who had risked everything to protect me.

"We do what we can," I said finally. "Where we are. With what we have." I gestured around the attic, at the evidence of his care—the books, the radio, the food he somehow procured despite wartime shortages. "This matters."

Fritz held my gaze for a long moment, something vulnerable and questioning in his expression. Then he nodded once, accepting what I offered even if it couldn't fully absolve him.

"It's late," he said, rising to leave. "Try to sleep. It's going to be hot again tomorrow."

His hand touched my shoulder as usual before he descended the ladder, but this time it lingered slightly longer, a wordless acknowledgment of what remained unspoken between us.

That night, as I lay on my mattress listening to the distant sounds of the city under curfew, I allowed myself to truly contemplate "after" for the first time since the bombing. What would remain for me in a post-war world? My family, if they still lived in Zeeland. Perhaps some distant relatives or friends who might have survived the ongoing roundups. But David was gone, the bakery destroyed, my identity as both a Jew and a homosexual still dangerous even if the Germans were defeated.

And what of Fritz? What place would exist for a German officer who had secretly harboured a Jew? Too compromised for acceptance among the victors, too traitorous for forgiveness from his own people. We were both men without countries, without clear futures.

Yet somehow, in the quiet darkness of the attic, this shared uncertainty felt like connection rather than isolation. Whatever came after, we were bound together now—the hidden and the hiding, the saved and the saviour, two men whose lives had become inextricably entangled by war's strange gravity.

As summer faded into autumn, a new element entered our precarious arrangement. One afternoon, while Fritz was at headquarters, I heard the front door open below. Instantly alert, I moved toward the hiding place he had built, prepared to disappear into the narrow gap behind the wall panel.

But the footsteps that entered were light, cautious—nothing like the heavy boot-falls of German soldiers. They moved directly to the kitchen, where I heard the soft clink of items being placed on a surface, then departed as quietly as they had come.

When Fritz returned that evening, I asked about the visitor.

"Ah," he said, a slight flush colouring his pale face. "That would be Mevrouw Jansen. From two streets over." He hesitated. "She brings food sometimes."

"Brings food?" I repeated, confused. "To a German officer's house?"

Fritz's flush deepened. "She thinks... that is, I've allowed her to believe..." He sighed. "She thinks the food is for a Dutch girl I'm involved with. Someone I'm keeping secret from my superiors because fraternization is discouraged."

I stared at him, processing this unexpected information. "And she helps with this? Why would a Dutch woman help a German officer with a romantic liaison?"

"Her son is in a labour camp in Germany," Fritz admitted. "I arranged better conditions for him. Food packages. Letters home." He met my gaze directly. "I didn't tell you because I wasn't sure you would approve of the deception."

I wasn't sure what to think. The arrangement provided additional food—explaining some of the mysterious extras Fritz had been bringing—but it also introduced a new risk, another person who might eventually betray us, deliberately or accidentally.

"Can she be trusted?" I asked.

"As much as anyone can be in these times," Fritz replied. "She believes she's repaying a debt. And she believes in romance, in human connection despite war." His mouth curved in a sad smile. "She sees me as a man first, a uniform second. That's rare enough to be valuable."

I nodded slowly, understanding. In a world determined to reduce people to categories—German, Dutch, Jew, Aryan—any recognition of common humanity became precious, worth preserving even at significant risk.

"Just be careful," I said. "For both our sakes."

Fritz's expression softened. "Always."

And so Mevrouw Jansen became an unseen presence in our strange household—the invisible provider of small luxuries, the unwitting supporter of a deception far different from the one she believed she was facilitating. Her deliveries continued through the fall and into winter, supplementing our meagre provisions as food grew scarcer throughout occupied Rotterdam.

By December 1941, the war had expanded yet again. The radio brought news of Pearl Harbour, of America's entry into the conflict, of a truly global struggle taking shape. The German broadcasts attempted to minimise these developments, but even their propaganda couldn't fully mask the significance of the United States joining the Allied powers.

"It will be years still," Fritz cautioned when I expressed hope that the end might be approaching. "America must build its forces, transport them across oceans. And our armies are still deep in Russia, still occupying most of Europe."

I knew he was right, yet the knowledge that the world's greatest industrial power now stood against Germany provided a comfort I hadn't allowed myself before. For the first time, I began to truly believe there might be an "after"—

that survival might eventually mean more than just continued hiding.

That Christmas Eve, Fritz surprised me by bringing a small pine branch and a single candle to the attic. He arranged them on the table, creating a miniature version of the Christmas trees that had once brightened Rotterdam's homes before occupation and rationing made such traditions impossible.

"It's not much," he said with the familiar apology that accompanied his gifts. "But I thought... it's still Christmas."

I was touched beyond words by the gesture—not because I celebrated the holiday myself, but because of what it represented. Normality. Tradition. The possibility of joy even in darkness.

"Thank you," I said simply.

We sat together in the candlelight, sharing a meal slightly more special than usual—real bread, a small piece of cheese, even a tiny cake Mevrouw Jansen had somehow procured. Neither of us spoke much, the moment too fragile for words that might break its strange peace.

When Fritz finally rose to leave, his hand rested on my shoulder longer than usual. I reached up, covering it briefly with my own—an acknowledgment of what remained unspoken between us, of the bond that had formed despite every force aligned against it.

"Merry Christmas, Arthijs," he said softly.

"Merry Christmas, Fritz," I replied.

He descended the ladder into the darkness below, returning to the world of occupation and division, while I remained in the attic that had become both prison and sanctuary. The candle burned on, its small flame defying the winter night.

For that brief moment, in the heart of occupied Rotterdam, in the attic of a German officer's house, a Jew in hiding found something unexpected—not safety, not freedom, but a kind of peace. Temporary, fragile, but real.

It was enough to sustain me through whatever still waited in the year to come.

CHAPTER 11: RAIDED

Rotterdam, 1942

I was reading Goethe when they came.

By the spring of 1942, I had settled into a routine in Fritz's attic—as much as one can settle into hiding. I had been there for over a year, my world shrinking to those slanted walls, the small dormer window with its blackout covering, and the hidden panel Fritz had built behind the chimney stack. The initial gratitude for space to stand and move had slowly given way to a different kind of confinement—more comfortable than the cupboard, but confinement nonetheless.

My German had improved significantly. I could now read Fritz's books without constantly consulting the grammar guides, could understand the radio broadcasts without struggling to decipher their meaning. Sometimes Fritz and I would speak in German during his evening visits, his accent precise and academic while mine remained stubbornly coloured by Dutch rhythms. These language lessons gave structure to our days, a purpose beyond mere survival.

That morning—April 17, 1942—had begun like any other. Fritz had left early for his duties, bringing me a small breakfast of coarse bread and thin coffee before departing. The spring air had filtered through the cracks in the attic walls, carrying the scent of rain and, faintly, blooming flowers from somewhere nearby. I had settled into my usual position on the mattress, back against the wall, knees drawn up to support the book of Goethe's poetry Fritz had first given me in the cupboard.

I was so absorbed in the rhythm of the German verse that I almost missed the first warning sign—the sound of a vehicle stopping outside, doors opening and closing with military precision. My body recognised the danger before my mind fully processed it, adrenaline flooding my system as I froze, ears straining to confirm what I already knew.

Boots on the pavement. Multiple sets. Moving with purpose toward the house.

I was on my feet instantly, book abandoned, moving silently as Fritz had taught me. No time to gather possessions. No time to erase evidence of my presence. Only time to disappear.

My fingers found the nearly invisible seam in the wooden panelling. With practiced movements honed through countless drills, I slid the panel aside and slipped into the narrow space between the attic wall and the chimney. I pulled the panel closed just as I heard the front door open below—not Fritz's familiar careful entry, but the assertive intrusion of those who had no need to ask permission.

German voices echoed through the house, sharp with authority. Orders being given. Questions being asked, though of whom, I couldn't tell. Had they captured Fritz? Was he with them? Or had they come while he was away, a surprise inspection he couldn't warn me about?

The hiding space was even smaller than I remembered from Fritz's demonstrations. My shoulders pressed against both sides, the rough bricks of the chimney warm against my back, the wooden panel inches from my face. I could barely breathe, partly from the confined space, partly from the terror gripping my chest.

Footsteps moved through the rooms below, methodical and thorough. Drawers being opened. Furniture being shifted. The systematic search of men who knew their business. I closed my eyes, focusing on controlling my breathing as Fritz had insisted I practice. Slow, shallow breaths. Silent breaths. The kind that wouldn't betray my presence even in the quietest moment.

"Durchsuchen Sie das ganze Haus. Lassen Sie keinen Raum aus." Search the entire house. Leave no room unchecked.

The voice was unfamiliar—older, more authoritative than Fritz's. A superior officer, perhaps. My heart, which had been racing, seemed to stop entirely as I realised the implications. This was not a casual visit. This was a deliberate search.

More footsteps. Heavier boots ascending the stairs to the second floor. Doors opening and closing. Then, the sound I had dreaded most—the creak of the attic ladder being pulled down.

I pressed myself further into the hiding space, though there was nowhere further to go. The chimney bricks scraped against my spine, but I welcomed the pain. It grounded me, kept me from the panic that threatened to overwhelm rational thought.

Light spilled into the attic as someone climbed the ladder. One set of footsteps. Then another. Two of them, moving into the small space I had occupied just minutes before.

"Was zum Teufel ist das?" What the hell is this?

My blood froze. They had found something. Evidence of my presence. The book? The radio? The breakfast dishes I hadn't had time to hide?

"Sieht aus wie Bücher. Vielleicht studiert er." Looks like books. Perhaps he studies.

A grunt of acknowledgment, then the sound of my mattress being overturned, of the small table being moved. They were thorough, these searchers. Professional. They would leave no possibility unexplored.

I had been standing completely still, but now a new problem emerged. My right leg, pressed awkwardly against the wall, began to cramp. A tingling sensation at first, quickly building to a painful tightening of the muscle. I bit the inside of my cheek to keep from making a sound, the metallic taste of blood filling my mouth.

"Hier ist nichts." There's nothing here.

The first voice again, impatient now. Footsteps moved across the attic floor, coming closer to my hiding place. I could hear the man breathing, could almost feel his presence on the other side of the thin wooden panel that separated us.

He knocked on the wall—a sharp, percussive sound just inches from my face. Testing for hollow spaces. For secrets. For me.

I didn't breathe. Didn't move. Existed as a ghost might, present but incorporeal, willing myself to disappear into the very wood around me.

The knocking continued, moving along the wall. It passed over the hidden panel without pause, the craftsmanship of Fritz's construction holding firm under scrutiny. Then it stopped.

"Was ist das?" What is this?

My heart lurched painfully.

"Der Schornstein." The chimney.

"Hmm." A sceptical sound. More knocking, this time on the bricks beside me. The vibration travelled through the wall, through my rigid body. "Scheint solide zu sein." Seems solid.

A moment of silence, stretching into eternity. Then, mercifully, footsteps moving away.

"Kommen Sie. Es gibt nichts hier oben." Come. There's nothing up here.

The light dimmed as they descended the ladder, their voices fading but still audible as they continued their search on the floors below. I remained frozen in place, not daring to move despite the agony in my cramping leg, the desperate need for a deeper breath, the sweat trickling cold down my back.

Minutes passed. Or perhaps hours. Time lost meaning in that narrow space, measured only by heartbeats and shallow breaths and waves of pain from my protesting muscles.

Then, finally, the sound of the front door opening and closing. Vehicles starting. Departure.

Still I didn't move. Fritz had drilled this into me repeatedly: "Never emerge until I give the signal. No matter how long it takes. No matter how sure you are they've gone. It could be a trap."

So I waited, the cramping in my leg spreading to my back, my shoulders, my neck. Waited through the silence of the empty house, through the distant sounds of Rotterdam continuing its occupied existence beyond these walls. Waited as afternoon light faded to evening dimness, as the temperature in my narrow prison dropped with the setting sun.

When I finally heard Fritz's key in the lock, hours later, I was barely conscious—a combination of pain, oxygen deprivation, and emotional exhaustion having pushed me to the edge of awareness. His footsteps moved frantically through the house, faster than his usual careful tread.

"Arthijs?" His voice, low but urgent, reached me through the wooden panel. "Bist du da?" Are you there?

I couldn't answer, couldn't make my parched throat produce sound. But I heard him climbing the ladder, his movements quick with worry.

Light flooded the attic again—lamplight this time, warmer than the harsh daylight of the searchers. Fritz's breathing was audible, his concern palpable even through the wall that separated us.

"Arthijs?" Softer now, uncertain.

With enormous effort, I managed to tap once against the panel—our signal, established months ago. I'm here. I'm alive.

The panel slid aside immediately, revealing Fritz's face, pale with fear and relief. "Mein Gott," he breathed, reaching for me as I half-fell from the hiding place, my stiff limbs unable to support me properly.

He caught me, lowering me gently to the floor, his hands moving quickly to assess my condition. "How long have you been in there? Since they came this morning?"

I nodded, my voice still trapped somewhere beyond reach.

"Eight hours," he murmured, his face tightening with something between anger and anguish. "Forgive me. I couldn't get away sooner. They kept us all at headquarters after the search, questioning us."

As sensation painfully returned to my cramped limbs, I managed to croak, "What happened?"

Fritz helped me to the mattress, which had been roughly thrown back into place by the searchers. "Suspicions. Someone reported unusual activity. Meals for two. Lights in the attic." His mouth thinned to a grim line. "They've been watching the house."

Cold fear washed through me again, sharper than the pain of returning circulation. "Mevrouw Jansen?"

"I don't know." Fritz shook his head. "It's possible. Or neighbours. Or just routine suspicion. The occupation administration has been increasing surveillance of its own officers lately. Looking for disloyalty."

He handed me water, supporting my head as I drank. The simple liquid felt like life itself flowing down my parched throat.

"Did they find anything?" I asked when I could speak more easily.

"They found everything. The mattress, the dishes, all of it." His voice tightened. "I had to come up with a story quickly."

I felt the blood drain from my face. "What did you tell them?"

A flicker of discomfort crossed Fritz's features. "I told them I've been bringing a Dutch woman here. An informant who provides intelligence about where Jews are hiding in the city." He looked away briefly. "I implied that she stays overnight sometimes, in the attic where no one would see her during curfew, and that she... performs certain Favors for me in return for protection."

I stared at him, trying to absorb this unexpected fabrication.

"I had to make it convincing," Fritz continued, his voice lower. "I spoke about her crudely, as if boasting to fellow soldiers. Said things about Dutch women being..." He couldn't finish the sentence, shame evident in his expression. "I tried to sound like the kind of officer they expect. The kind they would believe."

"Did they believe you?" I asked.

"Not entirely, I think. But enough to leave without pressing further. For now." Fritz ran a hand through his hair in a rare gesture of agitation. "They'll be watching more closely. There might be surprise visits to catch me with this fictional informant."

I glanced around the attic, noting the disarray left by the search. "What happens now?"

Fritz's expression grew serious again. "Now we must be even more careful. They didn't find evidence this time, but they're watching. The risk has increased." He hesitated. "It might be wise to consider moving you somewhere else."

"Where?" The question emerged more sharply than I intended. "The cupboard again? Another attic? Where in Rotterdam is safer than here?"

"Not Rotterdam," Fritz said quietly. "I've been making inquiries. Cautiously. There are people in the countryside who hide Jews on farms, in barns. Places less watched than the city."

I stared at him, understanding slowly dawning. "You want me to leave."

"I want you to survive." His pale eyes held mine, intense with an emotion I couldn't quite name. "If that means leaving, then yes."

The thought of starting over—of trusting new protectors, of adapting to yet another hiding place—exhausted me beyond words. But more than that, the thought of leaving Fritz created a hollow ache in my chest that had nothing to do with the hours spent in the hiding space.

"And if I refuse?" I asked.

Fritz looked away. "Then we continue as before. But with greater caution. Less comfort." His gaze returned to mine. "And probably higher risk."

I nodded slowly. "Then we continue."

"Arthijs—"

"No." I cut him off gently. "I've survived the bombing. The cupboard. This." I gestured toward the hiding place that had saved my life today. "I'll survive whatever comes next. Here."

What I didn't say—couldn't find words for—was that leaving Fritz now seemed impossible. Not just because he represented safety, but because he had become... what? Not precisely a friend. Not family. Something harder to define, forged in the crucible of shared danger and mutual recognition.

Fritz studied me for a long moment, conflict evident in his expression. Then he sighed, acceptance settling over his features. "Very well. We continue. But things must change."

The changes were immediate and severe. The books disappeared, deemed too risky to keep. The radio was hidden within the wall space rather than in the attic proper. My mattress was modified to fold and fit behind the panel, leaving no evidence of habitation when not in use. Meals became simpler, requiring less preparation, leaving fewer traces.

Most significant was the new protocol—at the first sign of approach, any approach, I was to disappear into the hiding space. No waiting to confirm danger. No gathering of possessions. Immediate, unquestioning concealment.

That night, after Fritz had helped restore the attic and ensure all evidence of my presence was removed or hidden, he sat beside me on the mattress. Both of us were exhausted—me from the ordeal of confinement, him from the stress of the search and its aftermath.

"I thought they had found you," he admitted, his voice so low I barely heard it. "When they took me to headquarters for questioning. I thought they had discovered everything."

I glanced at him, struck by the vulnerability in his expression. "What would you have done? If they had?"

Fritz was silent for a long moment. "I don't know," he finally said. "Denied everything, perhaps. Claimed ignorance. Or..." He trailed off, but I understood the unspoken alternative. Resistance. Violence. A futile, fatal last stand.

"Thank you," I said, the familiar words carrying the weight of all I couldn't express. "For the hiding place. For the warning drills. For everything."

His hand found my shoulder in the gesture that had become our ritual. But this time, something was different. His touch lingered, conveying a desperation we both felt but couldn't acknowledge directly.

"I should let you rest," he said, rising reluctantly.

I nodded, though rest seemed unlikely. My body still vibrated with fear, with the memory of those hours in the wall space, with the knowledge of how close discovery had come.

As Fritz descended the ladder, he paused, looking back at me with an expression I would carry with me through all the dark days to come.

"We survived today," he said simply. "Tomorrow, we begin again."

That night, alone in the attic that had nearly become my tomb, I dreamed of David for the first time in months. Not the nightmare of searching through ruins, but something quieter, more melancholy. We stood in Noah's bakery, sunlight streaming through windows that no longer existed, the scent of fresh bread surrounding us.

"You're still here," David said, his amber eyes warm with the love I remembered.

"I'm still here," I agreed.

He smiled, that radiant smile that had first drawn me to him across the flour-dusted workspace years ago. "Good. Keep going, Arthijs. Whatever it takes."

I woke with tears on my face but a strange calm in my heart. The raid had shaken me, had brought death closer than it had been since those first terrible days after the bombing. Yet somehow, I felt more determined than ever to survive—not just exist, but live to see whatever waited beyond this war, beyond this attic, beyond this necessarily unfinished chapter of my life.

Outside, Rotterdam continued under occupation. Inside, I continued in hiding. Both of us damaged, diminished, but enduring.

Both of us waiting for liberation that seemed as distant as the stars.

CHAPTER 12: SOLITUDE

Rotterdam, 1942-1943

Time moves differently in hiding.

After the raid in April 1942, my world contracted once more. The already austere attic became even more spartan—the books gone, the radio concealed, every trace of my existence tucked away behind Fritz's ingenious wall panel. My life shrank to fit this new reality, becoming as minimal and hidden as my physical surroundings.

Fritz had grown more cautious since the search, his visits shorter and less frequent. "They're still watching," he would explain, his voice low even in the privacy of the attic. "Not just me. All officers. Looking for signs of divided loyalty." The strain showed in the new lines around his eyes, in the increasing tightness of his mouth, in the way his uniform—once worn with reluctant precision—now seemed to hang slightly looser on his frame.

By summer, we had established new rhythms. Fritz would leave each morning while I still slept, returning briefly at noon when possible, then again in the evening. Our conversations had become more efficient, less exploratory—necessary information exchanged quickly, personal reflections kept to a minimum. The luxury of meandering discussion was another casualty of the raid.

"I've arranged more ration cards," Fritz might say, passing me a small packet. "Enough for two weeks."

"Thank you," I would reply, tucking them carefully away.

"If I don't return tomorrow, don't worry. There's a meeting at headquarters that may run late."

"I understand."

And that would be all. The evening ritual of his hand on my shoulder remained our most consistent form of communication—a brief physical connection in a relationship defined by necessary distance.

I missed our longer conversations, the gradual unfolding of thoughts and memories that had helped maintain my sense of self during the first year in the attic. But I understood the need for caution. We had come too close to discovery to risk anything beyond the essential.

So I turned inward, making my own mind the territory I explored when the attic's confines became too restrictive. I developed elaborate thought exercises to pass the endless hours—reciting poetry I had memorised, recalling in minute detail the streets of pre-war Rotterdam, reconstructing recipes from Noah's bakery ingredient by ingredient, step by step.

I created mental maps of places I had known—my childhood home in the Jewish quarter, the bakery where I had found both purpose and love, the harbour where David and I had sometimes walked on rare days off. In my imagination, I could move freely through these spaces, noticing details I had overlooked in real life, finding unexpected beauty in the most ordinary corners.

Sometimes, when the solitude pressed too heavily, I conducted silent conversations with those I had lost. With David, whose absence remained an ache that never fully subsided. With Noah, whose practical wisdom I desperately needed in this impossible situation. Even with my parents in Zeeland, whose fate remained unknown, letters sent but never answered.

"How would you handle this, Noah?" I would ask the silence, imagining his thoughtful expression, the way he would consider a question before answering.

"One day at a time," my memory of him would reply. "That's how we get through the impossible. One hour, one minute if necessary. Just until the next."

These imagined dialogues weren't delusions—I never forgot they were constructions of my lonely mind. But they provided company when real company was too dangerous to seek. They helped populate my isolated world with voices other than my own, with perspectives that challenged or comforted me when Fritz couldn't be there.

The attic itself became a character in my solitary drama—a presence with moods and voices of its own. I came to know every creak of its wooden beams, every variation in temperature as sun moved across its slanted ceiling, every small draft that found its way through invisible cracks. The space that had once seemed gloriously roomy compared to the cupboard now revealed its true dimensions—too small for pacing, too confined for real exercise, too exposed for comfort yet too hidden for connection.

Despite these limitations, I established routines to maintain both physical and mental health. Each morning began with careful stretches, modified to accommodate the low ceiling and need for silence. I would work through each muscle group methodically, remembering the exercises Fritz had taught me during our early months together, when his visits had been longer and less constrained by external surveillance.

Afternoons were for mental exercise—German vocabulary review, mathematical problems worked out in my head, historical dates and events recalled and organised. Without books, I relied entirely on memory, discovering reserves of knowledge I hadn't realised I possessed, while also confronting the gaps in my education with frustration and occasional despair.

Evenings were the hardest. As darkness fell and the house below me settled into night sounds, loneliness would descend like a physical weight. I would lie on my mattress—now stored behind the wall panel during the day—and listen to the creaks and sighs of the building around me, to the distant noises of occupied Rotterdam beyond the attic walls.

On clear nights, I could sometimes hear music from a neighbour's radio—faint melodies drifting through open windows in the summer heat or seeping through cracks in the winter cold. German songs mostly, approved by the occupation authorities, but occasionally something familiar from before the war. These fragments of music became precious gifts, brief reminders of a world where beauty still existed, where human expression hadn't been entirely crushed beneath the Nazi boot.

I began to count small mercies, tiny comforts that might once have seemed insignificant but now sustained me through the endless hours of solitude. The patch of sunlight that moved across the attic floor on clear days. The sound of rainfall on the roof, a natural music that masked my movements and provided a sense of connection to the outside world. The occasional bird that would land on the edge of the dormer window, visible as a shadow through the blackout material, a living creature unknowingly keeping me company for a few precious moments.

Most important were the sounds from below—Fritz's house speaking to me throughout the day. The water pipes that hummed when taps were turned on. The front door's distinctive creak. The third stair from the bottom that groaned under any weight. These noises formed a language I learned to interpret with increasing precision, telling me when Fritz was home, when he moved from room to room, when he paused near the attic ladder, perhaps considering a brief visit that circumstances often prevented.

I became attuned to sounds beyond our house as well—the rhythm of the German patrols passing on their regular rounds, the changing patterns of traffic as curfew regulations shifted, the distant church bells that continued to mark the hours despite occupation. These sounds anchored me in time and place, reminding me that there was still a world beyond my hiding place, a reality my isolation sometimes made me doubt.

By the autumn of 1942, nearly two years had passed since I was forced into hiding, adjusting to a life lived in quiet secrecy. My body had adapted to confinement in ways I hadn't thought possible, but my mind increasingly rebelled. I found myself having conversations with inanimate objects, assigning personalities to the spiders that occasionally found their way into my sanctuary, counting and recounting the wooden boards that formed the attic floor until the numbers blurred and lost meaning.

I was slipping, slowly but perceptibly, into a state where reality and fantasy blended at the edges. Not psychosis—I remained fundamentally aware of my situation—but a kind of waking dream state where time lost coherence and thoughts looped endlessly through the same narrow channels.

Fritz noticed the change during his increasingly brief visits.

"You're not sleeping," he observed one evening in October, his eyes assessing me with professional detachment that couldn't quite mask his concern.

"I sleep," I replied, though we both knew it wasn't entirely true. My nights had become fractured, consciousness never fully surrendering to rest, dreams and wakefulness bleeding into each other until I wasn't always certain which state I occupied.

Fritz frowned. "You need more than this." He gestured at the attic, at the hidden panel, at the entirely inadequate life I was living. "The mind requires stimulation as much as the body needs food."

"And what would you suggest?" I asked, unable to keep a hint of bitterness from my voice. "A stroll through Rotterdam? Perhaps a visit to the library?"

He didn't react to my sarcasm, understanding its source too well. Instead, he reached into his coat and withdrew a small package wrapped in cloth.

"It's not much," he said, the familiar apology accompanying his offerings. "But it might help."

Inside was a battered chess set, the pieces small enough to fit in my palm, the board barely larger than a book. Some of the pieces showed signs of repair—a knight with its head reattached, a bishop worn smooth by years of handling.

"It was my grandfather's," Fritz explained, his voice softening with memory. "He taught me to play when I was seven. Said it would teach me to think before acting." A ghost of a smile touched his lips. "I wasn't a very good student in that regard."

I ran my fingers over the pieces, feeling the smooth wood, the subtle differences in shape and weight. "I don't really know how to play," I admitted. "I understand the basic moves, but strategy..." I trailed off, oddly embarrassed by this gap in my knowledge.

"I can teach you," Fritz said. "When I have time." His expression darkened slightly at this acknowledgment of our increasingly constrained circumstances. "And when I'm not here, you can play against yourself. It's not ideal, but it engages the mind differently than just thinking."

That night, after Fritz had gone, I set up the chess pieces on the small board, arranging them according to the brief instructions he had provided. I studied their positions, the potential movements, the relationship between individual pieces and the whole.

"The pawns are the soul of chess," Fritz had said, quoting his grandfather. "They seem weak individually, but together, they shape the entire game."

I lifted a pawn, feeling its modest weight, seeing the slight discoloration where countless fingers had held it before mine. This small wooden piece had existed long before the war, had been touched by hands now perhaps dust, had participated in games whose outcomes were long forgotten. It would continue to exist after I was gone, after Fritz was gone, after this war had become nothing but history.

There was comfort in that continuity, in being part of something that extended beyond my current confinement. The chess set became a connection not just to Fritz and his grandfather, but to a tradition of human thought and interaction that transcended the artificial divisions of nationality and politics that had shaped my existence into its current form.

I began to play regularly, following Fritz's instructions, setting up challenges for myself that became increasingly complex as my understanding of the game deepened. I would play both sides, attempting to maintain the integrity of the contest despite knowing all the intended moves. It wasn't perfect—nothing about my situation was—but it provided the mental stimulation Fritz had correctly identified as critically lacking.

Winter descended upon Rotterdam with particular brutality that year. The attic grew so cold that breath formed visible clouds, and I spent most days wrapped in every blanket Fritz could spare. The hiding space behind the panel, while cramped and claustrophobic, at least retained some warmth from the chimney bricks. I found myself retreating there not just when danger threatened, but sometimes simply to escape the biting cold of the larger attic space.

Food became scarcer throughout occupied Holland as the war progressed and German requisitioning intensified. Fritz did what he could, sharing his own rations and occasionally bringing small extras, but we both lost weight as the winter deepened. Hunger became another companion in my solitude, its voice sometimes louder than my own thoughts, its demands more insistent than any external threat.

Yet even in this coldest, darkest season, small mercies continued to appear. Mevrouw Jansen, who had disappeared after the raid, cautiously resumed her deliveries, though less frequently and with greater secrecy. Fritz never confirmed whether she had been the source of the suspicion that led to the search, but her return suggested either her innocence or her repentance.

One evening in December, as I huddled near the concealed wall space attempting to absorb whatever heat the chimney might provide, I heard unfamiliar movements in the house below. Not Fritz's careful tread, but something smaller, quicker. I froze, immediately alert to potential danger, ready to disappear behind the panel at the first sign of approach.

Instead, an unexpected sound reached me—high, musical laughter. A child's voice, speaking Dutch rather than German, asking questions I couldn't quite distinguish. Then Fritz's voice, gentler than I had heard it in months, answering with a patience that seemed at odds with the tense, efficient man who now visited my attic.

The mystery was explained when Fritz came up later that evening, bringing a slightly more substantial meal than usual and news from the world below.

"Mevrouw Jansen's granddaughter," he said in response to my unasked question. "Five years old. Her mother was caught in a work roundup last week." His expression tightened. "Mevrouw Jansen has no one else to watch the child."

"Is it safe?" I asked, thinking not of my own security but of the little girl downstairs, innocently present in a house that would mean her destruction if my presence were discovered.

Fritz sighed. "Nothing is safe anymore. But the child knows only that I am a German who helps her grandmother. She's too young to understand more." He hesitated. "And too young to be left alone while Mevrouw Jansen works."

I nodded, accepting this new complication in our already complex arrangement. "What's her name?"

"Lena." Fritz's expression softened slightly. "She reminds me of my niece. Same age. Same way of asking impossible questions."

I hadn't heard Fritz mention family before, and the reference caught me by surprise. It was easy to forget sometimes that he had a life before Rotterdam, connections beyond our shared secret.

"You have a niece?" I asked, hunger for conversation, for any new information, overwhelming caution.

Fritz nodded. "In Hamburg. My sister's daughter." A shadow crossed his face. "I haven't seen her in almost three years. She probably wouldn't remember me now."

The wistfulness in his voice opened something in me—a recognition of the losses we had both suffered, different in nature but similar in their absoluteness. Fritz might be physically free to move through the world in ways I could not, but he too lived in a kind of prison, separated from family, from authentic connection, from the person he might have been had history taken a different course.

"She would remember," I said, not knowing if it was true but wanting to offer some comfort in our shared isolation. "Children remember more than we think."

Fritz's mouth curved in a small, sad smile. "Perhaps." He glanced at his watch, the brief moment of openness already closing. "I should go. Patrol tonight."

But as he turned to leave, he paused, looking back at the chess board I had set up near my mattress. "You've improved," he observed, studying the position of the pieces. "You're thinking three moves ahead now."

"I have a good teacher," I replied.

His hand found my shoulder in our usual farewell, but this time I reached up, briefly covering it with my own—an acknowledgment of the connection that persisted despite everything designed to sever it.

That night, as I lay on my mattress listening to the winter wind finding every crack in the attic walls, I found myself thinking of little Lena downstairs. A child caught in the same historical catastrophe that had shaped my existence, though she couldn't yet understand its dimensions or implications. A life beginning while so many were ending, a future still unwritten amidst so much destruction.

There was something hopeful in that thought, something that extended beyond my immediate circumstances. The world continued. Children grew. Life persisted, even in the shadow of occupation and genocide.

I fell asleep more peacefully than I had in months, my solitude temporarily lightened by the knowledge that below me, in the same house that hid my secret existence, a child dreamed the uncomplicated dreams of the young.

In the deepest part of my hidden life, as 1942 yielded reluctantly to 1943, I found an unexpected truth: even in total isolation, we are connected. To the past, through memories and objects like Fritz's chess set. To the present, through the sounds and rhythms of the house that sheltered me. And to the future, through children like Lena who would inherit whatever world emerged from the current darkness.

I was alone, yes. But not, perhaps, as completely alone as I had feared.

CHAPTER 13: THE OUTSIDE WORLD

Rotterdam, 1943-1944

The world came to me in fragments.

By 1943, I had been in hiding for nearly three years—first in the warehouse cupboard, then in Fritz's attic. My physical reality remained unchanged—the slanted ceiling, the hidden panel Fritz had built, the chessboard that had become my most consistent companion. But the world beyond Rotterdam, beyond Holland, beyond the walls that contained me, was transforming. I could feel it even before I understood it, like sensing a storm's approach through pressure changes in the air.

The first indications came through Fritz. In March 1943, he returned late one evening, his uniform unusually dishevelled, something raw in his expression that I had rarely seen before.

"What is it?" I asked, immediately alert to the change in him.

He didn't answer immediately. Instead, he paced the small area of the attic where standing upright was possible, his movements tense, contained. When he finally spoke, his voice was low, as if he feared being overheard even here, in the space that had become our private world.

"Stalingrad has fallen," he said. "The Sixth Army is destroyed. Over ninety thousand German soldiers taken prisoner."

The news was momentous—I knew enough from the propaganda broadcasts on the hidden radio to understand that the German advance into Russia had been presented as unstoppable, the capture of Stalingrad as inevitable. This reversal represented more than a military defeat; it was a fracture in the narrative of German invincibility that had dominated Europe since 1939.

"The reports on Radio Berlin are calling it a 'strategic withdrawal,'" Fritz continued, his mouth twisting with bitter irony. "A 'shortening of the line.' But the truth is circulating among the officers. It's a disaster, Arthijs. The beginning of the end, perhaps."

"The end," I repeated, the words both exhilarating and terrifying. I had been hiding for so long that the concept of an "after"—a world where Jews weren't hunted, where nations weren't occupied, where people like me might live openly—seemed almost mythical, like the promise of a land I had heard described but never expected to see.

Fritz stopped his pacing, his pale eyes finding mine. "Not yet," he cautioned, reading the hope in my expression. "The Reich is wounded, not defeated. There will be more violence, more desperation, before it truly ends." His voice dropped even lower. "And more danger for anyone they consider an enemy."

I understood his warning. The Germans might be losing ground in Russia, but their hold on Rotterdam, on all of occupied Holland, remained firm. If anything, defeats elsewhere might intensify their grip here, their determination to maintain control where they still could.

"What does it mean for us?" I asked, the question encompassing all the complexities of our situation—him, a German officer increasingly doubting his nation's cause; me, a Jew whose very existence was forbidden; the tenuous safety we had constructed through deception and shared risk.

Fritz's expression softened slightly. "It means we continue," he said simply. "One day at a time. But perhaps now with a horizon to look toward."

That night, after Fritz had gone, I lay on my mattress thinking about horizons. About the possibility, however distant, of a world after hiding, after attics and cupboards and wall panels sliding closed to conceal my existence. The thought was almost too vast to contemplate, like trying to imagine colour after years of darkness.

Yet the seed had been planted, and in the months that followed, it grew alongside the news that Fritz brought from the outside world. Whispers of Allied advances in North Africa. German retreats on the Eastern Front. Increasing resistance in occupied territories. Each piece of information was like rainwater to a parched plant, nourishing tentative hope while simultaneously reminding me how isolated I had become, how disconnected from the human drama unfolding beyond my small space.

The radio helped fill gaps in my understanding, though Fritz cautioned me to use it sparingly and only when he was home, in case unexpected visitors arrived. Even the German-controlled broadcasts, stripped of their propaganda, revealed changes in the war's course through what they didn't say, through the topics they avoided or minimised, through the increasingly strident calls for sacrifice and resistance against "foreign aggressors."

"Read between the lines," Fritz advised when I expressed frustration at the radio's obvious lies. "Listen for what they're not telling you. That's often where the truth hides."

It was a skill I developed through necessity, this ability to discern reality within deliberately constructed falsehoods. To recognise signs of German defeats in broadcasts claiming strategic victories. To sense Allied progress in warnings about "terrorist attacks" on the continent. To understand that the "final victory" promised with decreasing conviction was becoming less final, less victorious, with each passing month.

But the most reliable news came from Fritz himself, whose position gave him access to information unavailable to most Dutch citizens. In July 1943, he told me of the Allied invasion of Sicily. In September, of Italy's surrender and subsequent German occupation. In November, of the Tehran Conference where Roosevelt, Churchill, and Stalin met to coordinate strategy.

"They're planning the invasion of Western Europe," he said one evening in early 1944, his voice a mixture of dread and hope. "The British and Americans. It's only a matter of when, not if."

"Here?" I asked, unable to imagine armies fighting through the streets of Rotterdam, bombs falling again on a city that had barely begun to recover from the destruction of 1940.

Fritz shook his head. "France, most likely. Normandy or Calais." He hesitated. "But when it comes—if they succeed—

everything will change. The Reich will throw everything into stopping them. And if they fail..." He didn't finish the sentence. He didn't need to.

As news of the outside world filtered in, I noticed changes in Fritz himself. The confident German officer I had first met by the river, steady, controlled, carefully compartmentalised, was eroding, revealing someone more complex beneath the uniform. His visits to the attic, once crisp and efficient, became longer when circumstances permitted, more contemplative. He would sit with me in the dim light of the single lamp we allowed ourselves, playing chess or simply talking in low voices about everything except the most immediate dangers.

He spoke more of his childhood in Germany, of the Hamburg he had known before Hitler's rise—a cosmopolitan port city not unlike Rotterdam, with its own rhythms and traditions. He talked about his studies at university, his ambitions to become an engineer, to build bridges and buildings rather than serve in an occupying army. And occasionally, in moments of particular openness, he alluded to his own hidden self, the desires that had marked him as different long before his doubts about Nazi ideology had emerged.

"There was a professor," he said one night, his gaze on the chessboard between us but his mind clearly elsewhere. "In my second year. He taught architectural theory." Fritz moved a piece, not really seeing the game we were playing. "He had a way of looking at the world—at buildings, at spaces—that made you see everything differently. Made you understand that what seems solid is really just an agreement we make with each other, a collective story about how things should be."

I waited, recognizing the significance of this rare personal disclosure.

"He disappeared in '38," Fritz continued. "After the universities were purged of 'undesirable elements.' Jewish, they said, though I never knew if that was true." His eyes finally met mine. "I never even knew his first name. Never spoke with him outside of lectures. But I think he saw me—really saw me. And I think he knew what that understanding cost me."

In these quiet revelations, these glimpses of the person Fritz might have been in another time, another place, I sensed both a deepening trust and a growing burden. As the war turned against Germany, as the occupation's grip tightened in response, Fritz's inner conflict intensified. The uniform he wore, the role he played, became more difficult to reconcile with the man I had come to know in the attic's intimate confines.

"Sometimes I don't recognise myself anymore," he admitted in the spring of 1944, as rumours of the coming Allied invasion grew stronger. "When I give orders. When I enforce regulations I know are wrong. When I stand silent while others speak of victories I know are defeats, of righteousness I know is evil."

I had no easy answers for him. My own existence had been reduced to waiting, to survival, to the preservation of a self that sometimes felt more memory than reality. What counsel could I offer to someone facing active moral compromise, daily decisions that balanced pragmatic necessity against ethical integrity?

"You're doing what you can," I said, echoing words he had once spoken to me. "Where you are. With what you have."

Fritz smiled faintly, recognizing his own phrases returned to him. "Is it enough?" he asked softly.

I thought of the attic around us, of the life he had preserved at considerable risk to himself, of the small mercies he had provided that had kept me not just alive but human during years of isolation.

"For me, it is," I answered truthfully.

As 1943 turned to 1944, as the war's tide shifted perceptibly beyond our small realm, I found myself contemplating identity in ways I hadn't before. Who was I now, after almost four years in hiding? What remained of Arthijs van Leeuwen, the baker's apprentice who had loved David, who had worked the dough with flour-covered hands, who had walked freely through Rotterdam's streets?

The physical changes were obvious. My body had grown thinner, muscles atrophied from limited movement, skin paler from years without direct sunlight. My hair, which Fritz occasionally cut to maintain some semblance of normality, had begun to grey prematurely at the temples. I had aged beyond my years, as if time passed more quickly in confinement than in the outside world.

But the internal changes were harder to quantify. I had developed a vigilance that never fully relaxed, an awareness of potential danger that hummed constantly beneath conscious thought. My senses had sharpened in ways specific to my environment—I could distinguish Fritz's footsteps from any other, could detect the subtle shift in air pressure when the front door opened three floors below, could interpret the house's creaks and sighs like a language I had always known.

In some ways, I had become smaller—my concerns immediate and practical, my horizons limited by what I could see or hear from my attic sanctuary. Yet in other ways, I had expanded, my internal world growing more complex as my external world contracted. I had developed wells of patience I never knew I possessed, depths of resilience that continued to surprise me, and an appreciation for small pleasures that my former self would have found incomprehensible.

Most unexpected was my relationship with Fritz. What had begun as wary dependence—the hunted relying on an unlikely protector—had evolved into something neither of us had names for. Not quite friendship, with its implications of equality and free choice. Not family, despite the intimacy forced upon us by circumstance. Something unique to our shared experience, forged in secrecy and sustained by mutual need.

I recognised the danger in this attachment, the way it blurred lines that perhaps should remain distinct. He remained, despite everything, a German officer, part of the machinery that had destroyed my city, killed my people, separated me from everyone I had loved. And yet, in the closed ecosystem of the attic, he had become my entire world—my source of news, of human contact, of the small kindnesses that preserved my sanity.

Did I care for him because he was genuinely worthy of care, or because isolation had left me no other target for human connection? Did he protect me out of moral conviction, or to ease his own conscience in a role he had come to despise? These questions haunted me during the long hours alone, complexities that could neither be resolved nor dismissed.

Yet alongside these doubts, a simpler truth emerged: whatever its origins or nature, the bond between us had become essential to us both. I saw it in the relief that softened Fritz's features when he entered the attic after particularly difficult days at headquarters. I felt it in my own anticipation of his footsteps on the stairs, in the way conversation with another human voice restored parts of me that solitude eroded.

In a world intent on categorizing and separating humanity—Jew and Aryan, German and Dutch, normal and deviant—we had created a small space where such distinctions, while not forgotten, could be temporarily transcended. Where Fritz could be simply Fritz, not Lieutenant Neumann, and I could be Arthijs, not a hidden Jew or a number in a registry of the condemned.

This transcendence wasn't political or ideological. It didn't erase history or absolve responsibility. It was personal, imperfect, limited to the confines of our shared secret. But in a time when humanity itself seemed under assault, this fragile connection felt like resistance—not against any specific regime, but against the forces that would reduce us all to categories, to enemies, to abstractions rather than individuals.

One evening in late May 1944, as the anticipation of Allied invasion hung almost tangibly in the air, Fritz brought unusual news—not of military movements or political developments, but of a more immediate nature.

"I've been reassigned," he said without preamble, his expression unreadable in the attic's dim light.

My heart seemed to stop. "Where?" I managed, the single word containing all my fear.

"Nowhere yet. It's a standing order—all administrative officers are to prepare for potential deployment to France." He sat heavily on the edge of my mattress. "They're strengthening the Atlantic Wall, mobilizing reserves. They know the invasion is coming."

"When will you go?" The question emerged small, vulnerable in ways I rarely allowed myself to be anymore.

Fritz shook his head. "I don't know. It might be days or weeks. It might not happen at all if I can make myself indispensable here." His pale eyes met mine directly. "But I need you to be prepared, Arthijs. If it happens—if I'm sent away—arrangements will need to be made."

The possibility of Fritz leaving had always existed abstractly, but now it loomed as immediate, concrete. Without him, the attic would transform from sanctuary to trap. My survival, which had become so intertwined with his presence, would suddenly depend on new variables, new protectors, new risks.

"What arrangements?" I asked, forcing practicality to overcome the panic rising in my chest.

"Mevrouw Jansen knows someone in the countryside. A farmer outside Utrecht. He has hidden others before." Fritz spoke precisely, factually, though I could sense the emotion he was controlling beneath this professional exterior. "If I'm ordered to France, she will help you leave here. At night, by bicycle. The farmer will meet you at a predetermined location."

I nodded, absorbing these contingencies, these plans for a future neither of us wanted to contemplate.

"It won't come to that," Fritz added, a rare optimism in his voice. "The invasion, when it comes—I believe it will succeed. The Reich is stretched too thin, its resources depleted. Liberation may come before I'm forced to leave."

I wanted to believe him. Wanted to trust that the Allied forces gathering across the Channel would indeed breach Hitler's Atlantic Wall, would push through France into the Low Countries, would reach Rotterdam before Fritz was taken from me or I was discovered by others less inclined to mercy.

But years in hiding had taught me to prepare for the worst while hoping for better. To recognise that survival often hinges not on what we want to happen, but on our readiness for what we fear most.

"I'll be ready," I promised. "Whatever comes."

Fritz looked at me for a long moment, something unspoken moving behind his eyes. Then, with a deliberateness that made the simple gesture seem ceremonial, he extended his hand—not in our usual farewell touch on the shoulder, but palm up, an invitation.

I placed my hand in his, the contact sending an almost electric current through skin unaccustomed to such direct human touch. His fingers closed around mine, warm and solid and real in a world that had become increasingly abstract.

"Whatever comes," he echoed. "We face it as we have everything else. One day at a time."

Outside, beyond the attic's walls, beyond Rotterdam's occupied streets, beyond Holland's bordered vulnerability, the world was in motion. Armies gathered. Leaders planned. The machinery of war ground inexorably toward a culmination that would reshape the continent and determine the fate of millions.

Inside, we held on to what we had built together—a fragile refuge not just of physical safety but of human connection, preserved against all odds in the shadow of history's darkest hour.

One day at a time.

For now, it was enough.

CHAPTER 14: LIBERATION APPROACHES

Rotterdam, 1944-1945

Hope arrived in the summer like a distant thunderstorm—first barely audible, then growing stronger, until it became impossible to ignore.

It was June 6, 1944, when I first sensed something had changed. From my attic sanctuary, I couldn't see the streets of Rotterdam, but I could hear them. The rhythm of the occupied city had become as familiar to me as my own heartbeat—the measured tread of German patrols, the subdued murmur of Dutch civilians, the occasional vehicle rumbling past under strict fuel rationing. But that morning, the pattern shifted. Urgent footsteps. Vehicles moving faster than usual. Voices raised with an edge I hadn't heard in years.

When Fritz finally appeared that evening, his uniform was impeccable as always, but his eyes held a light I had almost forgotten existed.

"It's happened," he said simply, climbing into the attic and closing the hatch behind him. "The Allies have landed in Normandy."

The words hung in the air between us, monumental yet somehow insufficient to describe what they truly meant. After four years of occupation, after countless lives lost, after a darkness that had seemed eternal—the first real hope of liberation had arrived on French shores.

"How... how is it going?" I asked, my voice catching. I had learned to moderate my expectations, to protect myself from disappointment.

Fritz moved to sit beside me on the narrow mattress. "The Germans are claiming it's contained, that the Atlantic Wall is holding." A small, tight smile crossed his face. "But I've seen the classified reports. The Allies have established multiple beachheads. They're moving inland already."

I closed my eyes, allowing myself to absorb this news, to feel its implications ripple through my body. The invasion we had spoken of for months, the possibility that had sustained me through the darkest nights—it was no longer theoretical. It was happening.

"What does it mean for Rotterdam?" I asked. "For Holland?"

Fritz's expression sobered. "Not immediate liberation, if that's what you're asking. The Allies must secure France first. Push through Belgium. It could be months." He hesitated. "And the Germans won't surrender easily. Hitler has ordered all occupied territories to be defended to the last man."

I nodded, understanding both what he said and what he didn't say. The war was entering its final phase, but that phase might be the most dangerous yet—especially for those, like me, still hiding from an increasingly desperate occupier.

"And your reassignment?" I couldn't help asking. The possibility of Fritz being sent to France had hung over us like a shadow since May.

"Deferred, for now," he replied. "Administrative officers are needed here to maintain order. But if the situation in Normandy worsens..." He didn't finish the sentence. He didn't need to.

That night, after Fritz had gone, I stayed awake listening to the changed sounds of the city. There was an electricity in the air, a tension that seemed to vibrate through the very walls around me. Rotterdam was holding its breath, waiting to see what this new chapter would bring.

The weeks that followed brought a strange contradiction—as Allied forces pushed deeper into France, as Paris was liberated in August, as Belgium began to fall in September, the German grip on the Netherlands tightened rather than loosened. Fritz brought reports of increased checkpoints, stricter curfews, harsher penalties for resistance activities. The occupation forces, sensing their time was limited, seemed determined to extract everything possible from Holland before being forced to relinquish it.

"They're stripping the country," Fritz told me one evening in early September, his voice tight with controlled anger. "Food, fuel, industrial equipment—anything that can be transported back to Germany is being requisitioned. They know they can't hold on much longer, so they're taking what they can while they still can."

The effects of this final exploitation soon became apparent, even in my isolated attic. The food Fritz managed to bring grew scarcer, the portions smaller. The house below me turned colder as fuel for heating became almost unobtainable. Mevrouw Jansen's visits stopped entirely—

whether from impossibility or caution, neither Fritz nor I knew.

But alongside these hardships came unmistakable signs of German retreat. Fritz reported convoys moving eastward through Rotterdam—troops, equipment, and officials being pulled back to defend the Reich itself. The radio, which I now risked using more frequently, carried coded messages of Allied advancement that even the most stringent censorship couldn't entirely suppress.

"Some units are simply abandoning their posts," Fritz whispered one night in late September, checking over his shoulder despite the fact that we were alone in the attic. "Not officially. Not in large numbers. But it's happening. German soldiers slipping away in civilian clothes. Officers requesting transfers to positions closer to the Fatherland."

"And you?" I asked, the question emerging before I could consider its implications.

Fritz looked at me steadily. "I'm still here."

Those three words contained multitudes—loyalty not to the failing Reich but to the promise he had made to keep me safe, determination to see our shared ordeal through to its conclusion, perhaps even something more personal that neither of us had fully acknowledged.

By October, the sounds of distant artillery occasionally reached Rotterdam—the front lines of liberation drawing incrementally closer. The city's atmosphere changed perceptibly, anticipation and fear mingling in equal measure. The occupation forces grew simultaneously more brutal and more disorganised, their orders increasingly contradictory, their discipline fracturing under the strain of imminent defeat.

Then came the news that transformed hope into despair.

"The Allied advance has stalled," Fritz told me one grim evening in late October. "Operation Market Garden failed. Arnhem couldn't be held." His voice was flat, exhausted. "The British and Americans are focusing on securing Belgium and pushing into Germany. Holland—especially the western provinces—may not be liberated until spring."

The news hit like a physical blow. After months of building hope, of counting days until freedom, the realization that winter would come before liberation was almost unbearable.

"What does it mean for us?" I asked, echoing the question that had defined our existence for four years.

Fritz sat heavily on the chair beside my mattress, suddenly looking older than his years. "It means hunger," he said bluntly. "The Germans are calling for a rail strike to hamper their retreat. The Dutch Resistance has complied. But without trains, food can't be distributed properly. Combined with German requisitioning..." He shook his head. "It's going to be a very difficult winter."

He was right. As 1944 drew to a close, what became known as the Hongerwinter—the Hunger Winter—descended upon western Holland with merciless force. Temperatures plummeted to record lows. Canals froze. Food rations dropped to less than 1,000 calories per day, then lower still. People began to starve in what had once been one of Europe's most prosperous regions.

In our attic sanctuary, Fritz and I adapted as best we could. We abandoned any pretence of separate rations—whatever food he managed to secure, we shared equally. We spent more time in the narrow hiding space behind the wall panel, using the chimney's residual warmth to stave off the most bitter cold. We conserved energy, speaking less, moving only when necessary, our bodies learning a new economy of survival.

Christmas came and went with little acknowledgment. The small pine branch Fritz had brought the previous year was an impossible luxury now. Instead, we marked the day by sharing a single, hoarded sugar cube, dissolved in hot water—a celebration so minimal it might have seemed absurd in earlier times, but which now represented extravagant commemoration.

"Next Christmas will be different," Fritz said quietly as we sipped the sweetened water. "You'll be free by then. Perhaps even reunited with your family in Zeeland."

I nodded, though such futures had become almost too painful to contemplate. After so long in hiding, the concept of freedom had acquired an almost mythical quality—desired but somehow unreal, like a story told to children.

January 1945 brought news that renewed hope even as conditions worsened. Soviet forces were advancing rapidly from the east. The Ardennes Offensive—Hitler's last desperate gamble—had failed. The Reich was collapsing in on itself, fighting a war on multiple fronts with increasingly depleted resources.

"It's only a matter of time now," Fritz said, his voice barely audible over the howling wind outside the attic. "Months, perhaps. Not longer."

But time had become our enemy as much as the Germans or the bitter cold. Each day brought new reports of deaths from starvation throughout Rotterdam—first the elderly and the very young, then increasingly the previously healthy. Fritz himself had grown gaunt, his uniform hanging loose on his frame, his cheekbones sharp beneath pale skin.

I worried about him constantly. As an officer, he received better rations than Dutch civilians, but I knew he was giving much of his allocation to me. His position was also growing more dangerous—as the Reich's defeat became inevitable, those seen as collaborators or occupiers faced increasing hostility and potential reprisals.

"You should consider leaving," I told him one evening in February, forcing the words past the resistance in my throat. "Going back to Germany before the end. You could claim illness, request reassignment."

Fritz looked at me for a long moment, something unreadable in his pale eyes. "And leave you here? Alone?"

"The Allies will come eventually," I said, trying to sound more certain than I felt. "And there are still resistance networks. I could find help."

He shook his head. "No. I made a promise. I'll see this through."

I didn't argue further, selfishly grateful even as I recognised the increasing risk he took by remaining. We had come too far together to separate now, when the end—whether liberation or disaster—was finally in sight.

March brought the first real thaw, both literal and figurative. The bitter cold relented somewhat. Rumours of Allied airdrops of food reached even our isolated attic. German forces continued their gradual withdrawal, their presence in Rotterdam diminishing visibly according to Fritz's reports.

"They're establishing a defensive line further east," he explained. "Concentrating remaining forces. Rotterdam is becoming less strategically important as they focus on protecting German soil itself."

The implications were clear: liberation was approaching. Not as quickly as we had hoped when the Normandy landings first succeeded, but more certainly than ever before.

Yet with this growing certainty came a new anxiety that neither of us acknowledged directly—what would happen afterward? When occupation ended, when hiding was no longer necessary, when Fritz was no longer an officer of the occupying force and I was no longer a Jew in hiding—what would remain of the connection that had sustained us through these impossible years?

This unspoken question hung between us during Fritz's increasingly brief visits, adding a bittersweet edge to the hope that grew stronger with each passing day.

Then, on an unseasonably warm evening in early April 1945, everything changed.

Fritz arrived at the attic hatch without his usual careful signal. His footsteps on the ladder were hurried, almost frantic. When he emerged into the attic, I immediately knew something was wrong. His uniform was dishevelled, his normally precise appearance abandoned. His eyes held a wild energy I had never seen before.

"Fritz?" I rose from my mattress, alarm replacing the greeting I had been about to offer.

"It's happening," he said, his voice raw. "Full withdrawal from Rotterdam. All administrative personnel ordered to report to assembly points for immediate evacuation eastward."

The words hit me like a blow. Despite knowing this moment would eventually come, despite preparing for it mentally for months, the reality was still shocking.

"When?" I managed.

"Now. Tonight." Fritz ran a hand through his hair, a gesture of distress I had rarely seen from him. "I slipped away to warn you, but I can't stay long. If I'm not at the assembly point by midnight, they'll come looking."

A cold clarity settled over me. This was it—the moment we had feared and anticipated in equal measure. The final parting that had been inevitable from the first day Fritz had hidden me in the warehouse cupboard.

"What about me?" I asked, hating the smallness in my voice but unable to prevent it.

Fritz moved closer, his hands coming to rest on my shoulders. "The city will be unoccupied soon—perhaps within days. The Allies are expected to arrive shortly after." His grip tightened slightly. "Stay hidden until you're certain the Germans are gone. Then find the resistance. They'll be emerging openly as liberation approaches."

I nodded, absorbing his instructions while fighting the rising panic at the thought of facing these final days alone.

"I've left everything I could," Fritz continued. "Food. Water. The last of the fuel. It's not much, but it should be enough until liberation." He hesitated. "And I've left a letter for the Dutch authorities. Explaining that you were hidden here against your will. That I forced you to stay silent. It should protect you from accusations of collaboration."

The gesture—his willingness to accept full blame for whatever came after, to shield me from potential reprisals when the occupation ended—broke something in me. Tears I had managed to control throughout years of fear and deprivation now threatened to overwhelm me.

"That's not true," I said, my voice rough with emotion. "That's not what happened."

"It's what needs to be believed," Fritz insisted. "For your safety. For your future." His hands moved from my shoulders to briefly cup my face, the touch so gentle it was almost unbearable. "You deserve a life after this, Arthijs. A real life, not defined by what happened here."

I reached up, covering his hands with my own. "So do you."

A sad smile touched his lips. "Perhaps. But my path will be different. Germany has much to answer for. Those of us who served, even reluctantly..." He shook his head. "The accounting will be severe. And necessary."

We stood there for a moment, the understanding neither of us had ever fully articulated finally emerging into the open. Not just protector and protected. Not just German and Jew. Two men who had found something human in the most inhuman of times. Who had preserved each other's essential selves when everything around them had conspired to destroy such connections.

"I have to go," Fritz said finally, his voice barely above a whisper. "If I'm caught here now, after the evacuation order..."

I nodded, knowing what would remain unfinished between us. Knowing, too, that perhaps it was better this way—cleaner, simpler, less complicated for whatever lives awaited us after liberation.

"Fritz," I said as he turned toward the ladder. "Thank you. For everything. For my life."

He paused, looking back at me with an expression I would carry in my memory through all the years that followed.

"And you for mine," he replied softly. "The real one. The one worth saving."

Then he was gone, descending the ladder in quick, efficient movements that reminded me of the German officer I had first encountered by the river—precise, controlled, revealing nothing of the man beneath the uniform.

The attic hatch closed. His footsteps receded through the house below. The front door opened and closed.

And I was alone.

Outside, Rotterdam prepared for its final transition from occupation to liberation. Inside, I wrapped myself in the blanket Fritz had left, breathing in the faint scent of him that still clung to the fabric, and began the last, lonely vigil of my years in hiding.

Freedom was coming.

But first, one more goodbye.

CHAPTER 15: THE HOUSE OF GHOSTS

Rotterdam, 1945

The first thing I noticed was the silence.

Not the silence of the attic—that had been a heavy, suffocating thing, pressing down on me like a weight. This was different. This was the silence of absence. Of an empty house long abandoned.

Seven days had passed since Fritz's departure. Seven days of solitude more profound than anything I had experienced in my years of hiding. The sounds that had structured my existence—Fritz's footsteps, the opening and closing of doors, the quiet murmur of his voice from the rooms below—had vanished, leaving a vacuum that amplified every creak of the settling house, every distant explosion as the war's final acts played out beyond my walls.

I rationed the supplies Fritz had left with careful precision—the stale bread, the few potatoes, the small tin of preserved meat that represented unimaginable luxury in Rotterdam's starving winter. Each morning, I listened to the hidden radio at the lowest possible volume, straining to interpret news through layers of static and propaganda.

The Germans were retreating. The Allies were advancing. Liberation was imminent.

But "imminent" meant different things to those fighting and those hiding. To armies, it might mean days or weeks. To me, confined in an attic that had been both sanctuary and prison for nearly two years, it meant each hour stretching into eternity, each unexpected sound triggering the instinct to disappear behind the hidden panel Fritz had built.

On the seventh day, I heard something new—vehicles moving through the streets below, but not with the regimented precision of German military transports. There were shouts in Dutch, not the harsh commands in German that had dominated Rotterdam for five years. And then, something I had almost forgotten existed—cheering. The sound of celebration rolling through the streets like a wave, growing louder, more confident with each passing moment.

I moved to the dormer window, carefully peeling back the blackout covering just enough to glimpse the street below. A British tank rolled past, soldiers in unfamiliar uniforms walking alongside it. Dutch civilians emerged from houses, waving improvised flags, embracing the Allied troops, weeping openly in the May sunshine.

Liberation had arrived.

I sank to my knees, overwhelmed by the sight. After five years of occupation, after years of hiding, after endless days of fear and hunger and isolation—it was over. The nightmare that had engulfed Rotterdam, that had taken David and Noah, that had forced me into shadows and secrets, had finally ended.

Yet I remained in the attic, paralyzed by a new kind of fear. The world below had transformed while I had been hidden away. I had changed too, in ways I was only beginning to understand. The prospect of stepping out of hiding, of reclaiming an identity I had suppressed for survival, of rejoining a society that had been broken and remade in my absence—it was terrifying in its immensity.

Another day passed before I found the courage to descend. The celebrations continued in the streets, though tempered now by the grim realities of a city emerging from occupation and starvation. Relief organisations had begun distributing food. Military administrators were establishing temporary governance. The first tentative steps toward rebuilding had begun.

I gathered the few possessions that had accumulated during my hiding—the clothes Fritz had provided, the chess set that had preserved my sanity, the small notebook where I had written poems and memories that no one would ever read. I tucked them into a makeshift bundle, then stood at the attic hatch, staring down at the ladder that led to the house below.

For a moment, vertigo overwhelmed me. I had not descended these stairs in almost two years. Had not walked on surfaces that allowed more than a few paces in any direction. Had not moved through rooms without slanted ceilings and hidden panels.

Slowly, carefully, I placed one foot on the ladder. Then another. Each step a negotiation with gravity, with muscles unaccustomed to such movement, with the psychological barrier between hiding and emergence.

The second-floor hallway was silent and still. Fritz's bedroom door stood slightly ajar, revealing a space of austere functionality—a narrow bed with military corners, a small desk, a wardrobe standing open and empty. He had taken little when he left, I realised. Whatever personal possessions he had accumulated during his years in Rotterdam had been abandoned in the hurried evacuation.

I moved down the corridor, my fingers trailing along the wall for balance, my legs unsteady after so long in confinement. The other rooms on this floor were similarly spartan—a small bathroom, a linen closet, a room that might have been intended for guests but showed no signs of use.

The staircase to the ground floor seemed impossibly steep, a vertiginous descent that required all my concentration. I gripped the banister tightly, counting each step, focusing on the simple mechanics of movement to keep fear at bay.

And then I was there—standing in the front hall of the house that had been my world and my prison for two years. The space looked different from this angle, from this freedom of movement. Smaller than I had imagined from the sounds that had filtered up to the attic. Shabbier too, with dust collecting in corners and paint peeling from the walls.

I moved cautiously through the rooms, relearning spaces I had known only through auditory clues. The kitchen where Fritz had prepared our meagre meals. The sitting room where he had sometimes received German colleagues, while I hid breathless in the attic above. Each space familiar yet strange, known yet undiscovered.

It was in what appeared to be a small office near the back of the house that I found the first shock. Papers were scattered across the floor, pages torn from books and documents. Chairs were overturned, drawers yanked from their cabinets. And on the walls—

My breath caught.

Swastikas.

Painted in red, slashed across the faded wallpaper. Nazi propaganda posters still clung to the wood in some places, curling at the edges, their messages bold and hateful.

I turned slowly, my heart pounding.

This had been a Nazi house.

Not just the residence of a reluctant German officer, which I had understood Fritz to be. Something more official. Something more deeply embedded in the machinery of occupation. The posters were not personal decorations but administrative tools—notices of regulations, warnings against resistance, depictions of Jewish "characteristics" intended to aid identification.

I had been hiding in the attic of the enemy.

A tremor ran through me. My hands clenched into fists as I stepped forward, my gaze darting over the wreckage. What had happened here? Who had lived in these rooms while I had been nothing but a ghost above them?

Then I saw it.

A photograph, half-buried beneath a pile of fallen papers.

I bent down, my fingers trembling as I pulled it free.

Fritz.

There was no mistaking him—his sharp, aristocratic features, the pale blue eyes that had watched me in the dark.

He stood stiffly in his uniform, his expression unreadable, his cap tilted at just the right angle.

But it wasn't the familiar face that stopped my breath. It was the context. Fritz stood among a group of officers, all in similar uniforms, arranged in formal rows for an official photograph. At the centre was a man I recognised from propaganda broadcasts and newspaper photos—a high-ranking Nazi whose name I couldn't recall but whose significance was unmistakable.

This was no ordinary administrative assignment. This was no reluctant officer fulfilling required service. The photograph depicted some kind of special unit, an elite group within the occupation structure.

I sank onto the floor, my back against the overturned chair, the photograph clutched in my hands.

Fritz had hidden me in a Nazi house. He had protected me in the belly of the beast.

And then he had left.

The realization washed over me in waves. Fritz Neumann—the man who had saved me from the raid, who had built my hiding place, who had shared his meagre rations during the Hunger Winter—had been more deeply complicit in the occupation than I had allowed myself to believe.

But he had also risked everything to keep me alive. Had committed treason against his country, had violated every oath his uniform represented, had placed himself in mortal danger daily for years—for me. A Jew. The very embodiment of everything his regime had sought to destroy.

How could I reconcile these truths? The Fritz who had sat with me in the attic, playing chess by lamplight, his voice soft as he quoted Goethe from memory—was that the same man who had stood proudly among Nazi officers for this photograph? The Fritz who had brought me food when he himself was hungry, who had warned me of raids at risk to his own life—was that the same man who had served a regime that had murdered millions of my people?

I looked again at the photograph, searching Fritz's face for answers. His expression revealed nothing—the perfect military mask, revealing neither enthusiasm nor reluctance. Only his eyes, those pale blue eyes that I had come to know so well, held a hint of something beneath the surface. A reservation, perhaps. A private self kept carefully separate from the public role.

Or was I simply seeing what I wanted to see? Projecting the Fritz I had known onto the officer in the photograph?

The questions spun through my mind as I sat amidst the ruins of this house of ghosts. Outside, liberation continued—soldiers and civilians moving through streets gradually reclaiming normalcy, food being distributed, order being established. Inside, I wrestled with contradictions that defied simple resolution.

I thought of Fritz's final words to me—about the accounting that would come for those who had served the Reich, even reluctantly. Had he known I would find this evidence of his deeper involvement? Had he anticipated the confusion, the sense of betrayal I now felt?

Or had his departure been a different kind of protection—sheltering me not just from discovery but from the full knowledge of who he had been, what he had done while wearing that uniform?

I exhaled slowly, my grip tightening on the photograph.

The third truth, the one I had been avoiding even in my thoughts, finally surfaced: And I missed him.

Despite everything the photograph implied, despite the questions it raised about his true role in the occupation, despite the propaganda still hanging on the walls around me—I missed his presence. Missed his quiet voice, his careful movements, his hand on my shoulder in our wordless evening ritual.

What did that say about me? About what four years of hiding, of isolation, of dependency had done to my ability to judge, to condemn, to maintain the clear moral lines the war had supposedly been fought to defend?

I had no answers. Only the photograph in my hands, the empty house around me, and the bitter recognition that liberation had brought not the clarity I had hoped for but a new kind of confusion.

I rose unsteadily, tucking the photograph into my pocket. Whatever Fritz Neumann had truly been—reluctant soldier or committed Nazi, saviour or deceiver, or some complex combination that defied simple categorization—he had kept me alive when so many others had perished. That fact remained, immutable, regardless of what the photograph suggested about his wider role.

I moved through the house one final time, gathering what few useful items remained—a worn coat that might help disguise my too-thin frame, a half-empty tin of food overlooked in the kitchen cabinet, a pair of shoes that might replace my deteriorating ones if they could be made to fit.

At the front door, I paused, looking back at the place that had been my world for two years. The Nazi posters curling on the walls. The scattered papers bearing eagle insignias. The emptiness where Fritz had been.

I had been hidden in a Nazi house. I had survived in the heart of the enemy's territory. I had formed a bond with a German officer that defied every boundary the war had established.

All of these things were true. All of these things were part of me now, woven into whoever I would become in this new, liberated world.

I stepped outside, blinking in the spring sunshine that seemed impossibly bright after years of dimness. Rotterdam spread before me, damaged but free, its citizens moving with the tentative optimism of the recently liberated. I joined them, another ghost emerging from hiding, carrying invisible burdens and unanswerable questions.

The war was over. My hiding was over. But the reckoning—with what had happened, with who I had become, with the complex legacy of both gratitude and betrayal Fritz had left behind—that was just beginning.

I walked away from the house of ghosts, the photograph heavy in my pocket, toward whatever remained of the world I had once known.

CHAPTER 16: LOST YEARS

Zeeland, 1945-1952

The sea never stopped moving.

That was my first thought upon arriving in Zeeland in the summer of 1945. After years confined to the stillness of attics and cupboards, the constant motion of the water was almost overwhelming—waves rolling endlessly toward shore, receding, returning again with quiet persistence. The North Sea stretched before me, vast and grey beneath an equally grey sky, its surface rippled by a wind that carried salt and promises of rain.

I stood on the dike near my parents' small house, feeling unsteady despite the solid ground beneath my feet. Three months had passed since liberation—three months of chaos and adjustment as Rotterdam transformed from occupied territory to free city. Allied soldiers, relief workers, returning evacuees, and emerging resistance fighters had created a swirling human current that I found difficult to navigate after years of isolation.

Finding my parents had been surprisingly straightforward. They were still in the small coastal village where they had moved before the war, their lives disrupted by occupation but not destroyed. My father's health had declined, his once-precise tailor's hands now trembling with palsy, but they had survived—a miracle in itself during years when survival often seemed the exception rather than the rule.

Their reaction to my appearance had been complex—joy mingled with shock at my changed appearance, relief tempered by grief when I confirmed what they had already suspected about my brothers. Pieter had died during the Rotterdam bombing, his tailoring shop reduced to rubble with him inside. Jan had joined the resistance and disappeared in 1943, his fate unknown but presumed final.

"But you're here," my mother had whispered, her hands framing my too-thin face, her eyes taking in the premature grey at my temples, the sharp angles of cheekbones rendered prominent by years of insufficient food. "You came back to us."

I hadn't told them everything. Couldn't explain about the cupboard, the attic, the German officer whose contradictions I still struggled to reconcile. Some experiences defied articulation, existing in a space beyond language's capacity to convey. Instead, I had offered simplified truths—I had hidden. I had survived. I had come home when it was safe to do so.

Now, standing before the sea that had always defined Zeeland's existence, I wondered what "home" truly meant. Rotterdam, the city of my birth and youth, had been altered beyond recognition, its familiar landscapes transformed first by bombing, then by occupation, and now by the chaotic energy of reconstruction. This coastal village, with its weathered houses and stoic inhabitants, was my parents' refuge but not my own.

I belonged nowhere.

The realization settled over me with the inevitability of nightfall. I was a fragment displaced from its original context, a survivor disconnected from the world that had formed him. Not just by geography or circumstance, but by experiences that had reshaped me into someone unrecognizable even to myself.

"Arthijs?"

My father's voice pulled me back to the present. He stood several paces behind me on the dike path, one hand braced against his walking stick for support, the other raised to prevent his cap from being taken by the wind.

"It's getting dark," he called. "Your mother has supper ready."

I nodded and turned away from the sea. Dutifully following him back to the small stone house that represented my new beginning. One foot in front of the other. Survival continued, even after survival had been achieved.

The bakery in the village centre was nothing like Noah's shop in Rotterdam.

Where Noah's bakery had been warm with wood and golden light, this place was stark and utilitarian—stone floors, whitewashed walls, equipment that had survived the war through sturdiness rather than care. The owner, Hendrik Visser, was similarly pragmatic—a large, taciturn man whose conversation rarely extended beyond necessary instruction or terse evaluation.

"You know bread," he had acknowledged after observing my work during the first week. It was neither compliment nor criticism, simply recognition of fact.

I had been fortunate to find employment so quickly. Skilled labour was in demand as the Netherlands rebuilt itself, and bakers particularly so. The country was still recovering from the Hunger Winter, still reliant on Allied food supplies and rationing. Those who could transform simple ingredients into sustenance were valued, regardless of their past or personal circumstances.

My hands remembered what my mind sometimes wanted to forget—the feel of dough, the rhythms of kneading, the perfect moment when bread was ready for the oven. These physical memories carried me through days when speaking felt impossible, when human interaction seemed a code I could no longer decipher.

Work provided structure. Structure kept the darkness at bay. Most days.

There were other moments, of course. When the clang of a dropped pan would trigger memories of bombs falling. When a customer's German-accented Dutch would freeze my hands mid-task. When the cramped supply closet would suddenly transform in my mind to the cupboard where I had first hidden, walls seemingly closing in until breathing became difficult.

Visser noticed but said nothing. Perhaps he had his own war stories, his own triggers and terrors. In those early post-war years, trauma was the Netherlands' most abundant crop, harvested from fields sown with five years of occupation, resistance, hiding, hunger, and loss.

"You should join us for the festival," Visser said one afternoon in the spring of 1946. It was the longest nonwork-related conversation he had initiated in the nine months I had been employed at his bakery.

"Festival?" I echoed, looking up from the rye loaves I was scoring.

"Queen's Day." He gestured vaguely toward the village square visible through the shop's front window. "The whole village celebrates. First proper one since before the war."

I nodded noncommittally, returning my attention to the bread. Social gatherings remained difficult—too many people, too much noise, too much unpredictability. I had constructed a life of controlled parameters: work, home, occasional solitary walks along the sea. Anything beyond this carefully maintained routine felt dangerous, exposing.

But my mother had been gently persistent in her encouragement to "rejoin the world," as she put it. My father, whose health continued to decline, said less but watched me with worried eyes that reminded me uncomfortably of Fritz in those final days before his departure.

So when Queen's Day arrived, I found myself standing awkwardly at the edge of the village square, watching as neighbours who had endured occupation together now celebrated their restored freedom and national identity. Orange decorations brightened the normally austere buildings. Music—folk songs long suppressed under German rule—filled the air. Children too young to remember life before occupation ran laughing through the crowd, their innocence both painful and precious to observe.

"They're resilient, aren't they?"

The voice came from beside me, female and lightly accented. I turned to find a young woman approximately my age, her dark hair pulled back simply, her dress practical but brightened with an orange ribbon in the day's spirit.

"The children," she clarified when I didn't immediately respond. "They adapt. They heal. Faster than we do, I think."

"Yes," I managed, discomfort at unexpected conversation warring with ingrained politeness. "They do."

She extended her hand. "I'm Hannah Bakker. You're the new baker's assistant, yes? Arthijs van Leeuwen?"

I nodded, briefly taking her offered hand. In a village this size, anonymity was impossible, though I had done my best to maintain as low a profile as possible.

"I teach at the school," she continued. "The little ones. Many of them mention the special bread rolls you make for them—the ones shaped like animals."

I felt heat rise in my face. The animal-shaped rolls were a small indulgence, a technique David had taught me years ago. Creating them for the village children had been an impulse I hadn't examined closely—a connection to memory that didn't hurt, perhaps, or simple pleasure in bringing joy to those who had known too little of it.

"It's not much," I said. "Just scraps of dough, really."

Hannah's smile suggested she understood more than I had articulated. "Small kindnesses matter. Especially now." She glanced around the celebrating square. "Everyone here is carrying something invisible. Wounds that don't show. Memories they can't speak about."

The insight surprised me, as did the ease with which she voiced it. Most people in the village maintained a determined forward focus, the past relegated to occasional commemorations but rarely discussed directly.

"You sound like you understand that well," I said carefully.

A shadow crossed her expression. "I was in Amsterdam during the occupation. Jewish Quarter." She didn't elaborate, didn't need to. The Amsterdam deportations had been particularly thorough, particularly ruthless.

"I'm sorry," I said, the words inadequate but heartfelt.

She nodded, accepting both the sentiment and its limitations. "Three years in an attic. Family that owned the house below hid me. Good people." A small, sad smile. "I was the only one from my family to survive."

The parallel to my own experience was so unexpected, so precise, that for a moment I couldn't respond. Here was someone who might actually understand—the confinement, the dependence on others for survival, the complex gratitude and guilt of being the one who remained when others perished.

"I was hidden too," I found myself saying, the admission slipping past defences worn thin by surprise and recognition. "In Rotterdam. First in a cupboard, then an attic."

Hannah's eyes met mine, and in that moment something shifted—a door opening between two sealed rooms, allowing air to circulate again. "How long?" she asked simply.

"Almost four years."

She exhaled softly. "Three years and seven months for me."

We stood in silence then, the festival continuing around us, its sounds and colours momentarily secondary to the quiet recognition flowing between two people who had lived parallel lives in different cities, who had emerged from hiding to find a world simultaneously familiar and unrecognizable.

"It gets better," Hannah said finally. "Not perfect. Not like before. But better."

I wanted to believe her. Wanted to trust that time would eventually soften the sharp edges of memory, would allow me to exist in the present without being constantly pulled back into the past. That someday I might attend a festival without positioning myself near exits, might hear German spoken without tensing, might sleep through the night without waking to check that my hiding place remained secure.

"How?" I asked, the single word containing all my doubt.

Hannah considered this, her gaze moving back to the celebrating villagers. "By allowing yourself to be part of things again. Little by little." She smiled faintly. "By making bread-roll animals for children. By standing at festivals even when you'd rather be alone. By remembering that survival itself was an act of resistance, and continuing to survive—to truly live—is how that resistance continues."

Her words found purchase in places within me that had been carefully walled off, introducing questions I had avoided since emerging from hiding. What did survival mean beyond the immediate preservation of life? What responsibilities came with being one of the few who remained when so many had been lost?

Before I could respond, a group of children spotted Hannah and rushed toward her with the uncomplicated enthusiasm of the young. She greeted them warmly, shifting seamlessly from our weighty conversation to their simple excitement over the day's festivities.

"Come find me again," she said over her shoulder as the children pulled her toward a game being organised near the village hall. "If you want to talk more."

I watched her go, feeling simultaneously relieved and bereft. The brief connection had been both unsettling and comforting—a reminder that I was not as alone in my experiences as I had believed, yet also a confrontation with parts of myself I had carefully avoided examining.

That night, I dreamed of David for the first time in months. Not the nightmare of searching through Rotterdam's ruins, but something quieter—the two of us in Noah's bakery, working side by side in the golden morning light. When I woke, the loss felt freshly raw, but alongside it was something unexpected: gratitude for having known him, for having experienced love in a world determined to deny it.

Perhaps Hannah was right. Perhaps healing began with allowing oneself to remember without being consumed by the remembering. To acknowledge loss without being defined by it. To recognise that surviving carried with it an obligation to those who hadn't—the obligation to live fully, consciously, meaningfully.

The next day, I shaped twice as many animal rolls for the village children.

Life in Zeeland settled into patterns dictated by season and necessity. The immediate post-war recovery gave way to more stable rebuilding as the Netherlands gradually reclaimed its place in a transformed Europe. Rationing ended. Businesses expanded. A cautious prosperity began to emerge from the ashes of conflict.

By 1949, I had advanced from assistant to head baker at Visser's shop, the older man's hands increasingly troubled by arthritis. The promotion brought additional responsibilities but also creative freedom—the ability to introduce recipes and techniques I had learned from Noah and David in the Rotterdam bakery that no longer existed.

My father did not live to see this small professional triumph. His health, precarious since before the war, failed entirely in the harsh winter of 1948. I buried him in the small churchyard overlooking the sea he had come to love in his final years, my mother's quiet grief adding another layer to the accumulated losses that defined our family's history.

Hannah Bakker remained in the village, our initial connection evolving into something like friendship—tentative at first, then gradually more comfortable as we discovered shared interests beyond our parallel experiences of hiding. She understood, as few others could, the complex aftermath of prolonged isolation. The discomfort with open spaces after years of confinement. The hypervigilance that never entirely disappeared. The difficulty of explaining to others what felt fundamentally inexpressible.

"Do you ever wonder about the people who hid you?" she asked one evening as we walked along the dike path. It was autumn 1951, the air crisp with the promise of approaching winter. "The family in Amsterdam. I visit them sometimes, but it's... complicated."

I hesitated, the familiar knot forming in my stomach at the thought of Fritz Neumann. In all our conversations, I had never fully explained the nature of my hiding place—had spoken of "someone who helped me" without specifying that this someone had worn a German uniform, had been part of the very machinery of occupation we had been hiding from.

"I don't know what happened to him," I said finally. "He left when the Germans evacuated Rotterdam. Before liberation."

Hannah glanced at me, perhaps noting the deliberate omission in my response, but didn't press. She had her own silences, her own carefully maintained boundaries around certain aspects of her wartime experiences.

"I wonder sometimes if we ever really leave those hiding places," she said instead. "Physically, yes. But here..." She tapped her temple gently. "Part of me is still in that Amsterdam attic. Still holding my breath when footsteps approach. Still counting floorboards to pass the time."

I nodded, understanding exactly what she meant. "The hiding becomes part of you."

"But not all of you," she added, her voice firm. "That's what I try to remember on the difficult days. It shaped me, but it doesn't define me. Not completely."

Her words echoed in my mind later that night as I prepared for bed in the small house I had purchased the previous year. My mother had moved in with her sister in a neighbouring village, finding comfort in family connections as she adjusted to widowhood. I had chosen to remain in the coastal community that had become, if not home exactly, then at least a place where I understood my role and purpose.

The house was modest but suited my needs—a bedroom, a small sitting room, a kitchen where I sometimes experimented with recipes too elaborate for the bakery's commercial constraints. There were no attics, no hidden panels, no cupboards large enough for a man to hide in. I had chosen it for these absences as much as for its positive qualities.

Yet Hannah was right. The hiding places remained within me, architectural features of an interior landscape permanently altered by years of concealment and fear. I carried them as surely as I carried the memories of those I had lost—David, Noah, my brothers, my father. As surely as I carried the complicated legacy of Fritz Neumann, whose contradictions I still struggled to reconcile each time I recalled his face.

What I hadn't fully acknowledged, even to myself, was how these internal hiding places had prevented me from truly engaging with the life I had been so desperate to preserve. I had survived—a miracle in itself given how many hadn't—

but survival had remained my primary goal even years after the immediate danger had passed. I existed carefully, cautiously, containing myself within boundaries as rigid as any hiding spot's walls.

I stood at my kitchen window, looking out at the night sky above Zeeland's flat landscape. Stars punctured the darkness, their light ancient yet immediate, a reminder of continuity beyond human tragedy and triumph. Somewhere beneath those same stars was Fritz, if he still lived. And David, in whatever form existence took after life ended. And all the others whose paths had crossed mine before war had scattered us to separate fates.

For the first time, I allowed myself to fully feel the emptiness of having survived alone. Not just the specific absences of individuals, but the broader isolation of being disconnected from my past, from the person I had been before hiding, from the community that had once given my existence context and meaning. The grief, when it came, was not the sharp agony of fresh loss but something deeper—a recognition of all that could never be recovered, all that would always remain incomplete.

Yet within that recognition was the beginning of something else. The understanding that life continued despite its fractures. That meaning could be found even in fragmentation. That surviving alone did not necessarily mean living alone.

The next morning, I rose before dawn as usual, preparing for another day at the bakery. But as I walked through the quiet village, the stars still visible above me and the first hint of grey touching the eastern horizon, I felt a subtle shift—like a door long sealed finally beginning to open, allowing fresh air into rooms too long closed.

I carried my history with me, yes. The cupboard. The attic. The years of isolation and fear. But perhaps the time had come to build something new around these unchangeable facts—not to erase them or deny them, but to integrate them into a life that extended beyond mere continuation. Beyond simple survival.

The sea never stopped moving. Perhaps I could learn from its example—to remain in motion despite what had been lost, to continue forward while carrying the past, to find strength in the very rhythms that had once seemed overwhelming.

It wasn't healing, exactly. Some wounds were too fundamental for complete recovery. But it was, perhaps, the beginning of living deliberately in the aftermath. Of choosing to exist fully in whatever time remained.

Of recognizing that the lost years needn't define those still to come.

CHAPTER 17: THE FLOOD

Zeeland, 1953

By 1953, I had built a life in Zeeland. A quiet life.

I didn't speak much of the war. Not to the people in the village, not to the few acquaintances I had made over the years. It had settled inside me like an old wound—scarred over, but never quite forgotten.

The sea had always been my constant. I found work in a small bakery again, kneading dough before dawn, the scent of fresh bread filling the air as the first fishermen came in from the harbour. It was a good life, simple and steady.

Then came the flood.

I remember that Saturday, the 31st of January, with the clarity that only precedes disaster. The day had begun with an unsettled sky—dark clouds scudding across the horizon, driven by winds that seemed to gather strength with each passing hour. By afternoon, those winds had become a gale, howling around the corners of buildings and rattling the windows of my small house near the dike.

"Storm coming," old Visser had commented as we finished the day's baking. "A bad one, by the feel of it."

I had nodded, helping him secure the shutters before making my way home through streets already emptying as villagers sought shelter. The air held that peculiar electric tension that precedes significant weather events—a pressure against the skin, a heaviness in each breath. The sea, visible beyond the dike, had turned an ominous grey-green, its surface whipped into white-capped fury by the strengthening winds.

That evening, as darkness fell, the storm intensified. Rain lashed against my windows with a violence that seemed personal, as if the water itself harboured some grudge against the structures we had built to keep it at bay. The wind's howl became a constant presence, rising occasionally to screams that made me think, irrationally, of the air raid sirens in Rotterdam so many years before.

I had lived through storms in Zeeland before. The region's position, caught between the North Sea and the mouths of three major rivers, made it vulnerable to nature's more dramatic moods. But there was something different about this one—a sustained intensity, a relentlessness that stirred old anxieties I had thought long buried.

Unable to sleep, I sat by my front window, watching the rain drive horizontally across my small garden. The house creaked and shuddered around me, but I took comfort in its solid construction, in the generations of Zeelanders who had built these stone dwellings to withstand the sea's periodic rages.

Just after midnight, as January yielded to February, a sudden pounding at my door startled me from my weather-watching vigil.

It was Jan Dekker, the village council head, his raincoat streaming water onto my floor as he stepped inside without waiting for an invitation.

"The dike is failing," he said without preamble, his voice tight with controlled fear. "North of the village. Water's coming over the top already. We're evacuating everyone to the church on high ground."

The words struck me with physical force. The dikes were Zeeland's primary protection, the only barrier between habitable land and the hungry sea. Their failure was the nightmare scenario every coastal resident lived with but rarely acknowledged.

"How much time?" I asked, already moving to gather essentials.

"Minutes, not hours," Dekker replied grimly. "Take only what you need to survive. Leave the rest."

He was gone before I could ask more, hurrying to the next house with his warning. I moved with the efficiency born of past crises, packing a small bag with clothes, my identification papers, and the few irreplaceable mementos I had managed to salvage from my previous life—my father's pocket watch, a photograph of my family taken before the war, the chess piece Fritz had given me when we parted.

The thought of Fritz surfaced unexpectedly as I prepared to abandon my home. Where was he now? Had he survived the aftermath of Germany's defeat? Did he ever think of the Jewish man he had hidden in his attic for those long years? Questions without answers, particularly now as a more immediate threat demanded my attention.

Outside, the village had transformed into a scene of controlled chaos. Families hurried through the storm-lashed darkness, parents carrying small children, older residents supported by neighbours. The wind tore at clothing and voices alike, making communication nearly impossible except through gestures and physical guidance. The church bell rang continuously, its urgent peals barely audible above the storm but providing a direction for those disoriented by darkness and fear.

I joined the flow of evacuees, helping where I could—steadying an elderly woman when she stumbled, carrying a child whose mother was already burdened with an infant and belongings. The solidarity was immediate and unquestioned, the village becoming in crisis what it always claimed to be in peace—a community where each supported all.

As we neared the church, built providentially on the highest point in the area, a new sound cut through the storm's roar—a deep, rushing noise that seemed to vibrate through the ground beneath our feet. I turned, as did many others, toward the northern edge of the village where the dike had stood for generations.

Even through the darkness and driving rain, the disaster was visible. The dike had not merely been overtopped—it had been breached. A massive section had given way, and through the gap, the North Sea was pouring into Zeeland with unstoppable force. The water moved not like the familiar tides but like something alive and hungry, swallowing streets and gardens, surrounding homes, advancing with terrifying speed toward the centre of the village.

"Run!" someone shouted, unnecessary but instinctive in the face of such primal danger.

We ran, all pretence of order abandoned as survival instinct took control. The church loomed ahead, its sturdy stone walls and elevated position offering the only realistic refuge. Behind us, the flood continued its inexorable advance, water already ankle-deep in the streets we had just traversed.

I reached the church steps, turning to help others up the increasingly slippery stone. The scene before me burned itself into memory—villagers struggling through rising water, the distant shapes of homes now standing in a newly formed lake, the continued collapse of the dike releasing even more of the sea into our fragile human settlement.

Inside the church, hundreds of people huddled in pews and aisles, their faces painted with equal measures of relief at temporary safety and fear of what morning might reveal. Children cried, adults spoke in hushed voices, and the building itself seemed to strain against the wind that battered its ancient stones and rattled its stained-glass windows.

Pastor Vos moved among the refugees, offering what comfort he could through presence rather than platitudes. When he reached me, he paused, his weathered face grave in the lantern light.

"It's not just our village," he said quietly. "Reports were coming in by telephone before the lines went down. The entire coast is affected. Many dikes breached. Islands completely underwater." He glanced toward the windows, beyond which the storm continued unabated. "This is unprecedented."

The word hung in the air between us, heavy with implication. The Dutch had fought the sea for centuries, had developed sophisticated systems of dikes and pumps, had reclaimed land and held it against nature's periodic attempts to reclaim it. "Unprecedented" meant those systems had failed. Meant we faced something beyond our collective experience and preparation.

I thought of Rotterdam then—of how quickly the familiar could be destroyed, of how permanently a landscape could be altered by forces beyond human control. First bombs, now water. Different agents of destruction but similar in their capacity to erase what we foolishly considered permanent.

The night passed with agonizing slowness. The storm showed no signs of abating, its fury sustained rather than peaking and diminishing. Occasionally, someone would venture to a window and report on the water's progress—rising steadily, surrounding the church, transforming the village into an archipelago of rooftops jutting from a newly formed sea.

By dawn, a grey light filtering through still-heavy clouds, the full scope of the disaster began to reveal itself. The water had stabilised at a depth of nearly two meters in the lower parts of the village. Many smaller homes stood with only their roofs above water. The stronger stone buildings, like my own, had weathered the initial flood but were now islands accessible only by boat—if boats could be found.

And still the storm continued, though with slightly diminished strength as morning advanced. We could see now what we had only heard in darkness—the debris carried by the floodwaters, the occasional livestock carcass, the family possessions bobbing absurdly on the surface of what had been streets and gardens mere hours before.

Pastor Vos organised us into action teams—those tending to the elderly and children, those inventorying our collective food supplies, those monitoring the flood levels and structural integrity of our refuge. I joined the latter group, my experience in Rotterdam having taught me something about assessing damaged buildings.

"It will hold," I assured the pastor after examining the church's foundations where they now met the floodwaters. "These walls have stood for centuries. They won't yield to one night's storm."

He nodded, the relief in his eyes betraying the fear he had kept from his voice when addressing the congregation. "And the water? Still rising?"

I shook my head. "Stable for the last hour. If the dike doesn't breach further, we may have seen the worst."

But "the worst" was relative. Even if the waters receded immediately—which seemed unlikely given the storm's continued presence—the damage was catastrophic. Homes destroyed or rendered uninhabitable. Farmland inundated with salt water that would take years to flush from the soil. Livestock drowned. Livelihoods swept away as completely as the physical structures that had supported them.

By midday, the first rescue efforts began to reach us. Boats from less affected areas navigated the flooded streets, taking the most vulnerable—the elderly, the injured, young children and their mothers—to higher ground beyond the village where military transport waited to evacuate them further inland.

I helped coordinate the loading of boats, using the village council's list to ensure no one was overlooked in the confusion. It was familiar work in its way—the methodical organisation required during crisis, the need to remain calm when others couldn't, the focus on immediate necessities rather than long-term implications.

It was during one such loading operation, as I helped an elderly couple into a fishing boat that would take them to the evacuation point, that I first noticed him.

He stood on the far side of what had been the village square, now a rippling expanse of grey-brown water. Taller than most of the Dutch rescuers, his fair hair visible despite being darkened by rain and plastered against his head. He was helping guide another boat toward a partially submerged home where figures could be seen at an upper window.

I froze, my hand still extended toward the elderly woman I had been assisting.

It couldn't be. It was impossible.

Yet something in his movements, in the set of his shoulders, in the efficient way he directed the rescue operation without raising his voice—it was achingly, impossibly familiar.

"Are you all right, young man?" the elderly woman asked, her concern pulling me back to the immediate task.

"Yes," I managed, helping her settle on the boat's bench. "Yes, I'm fine. Safe journey."

As the boat pulled away, I remained rooted in place, my eyes fixed on the distant figure. He turned slightly, his profile becoming visible for a moment before he moved to help someone into the boat he had been guiding.

My heart seemed to stop, then resume at double speed.

Fritz.

After eight years. After the collapse of the Reich he had served. After the liberation and reconstruction and all the small daily moments that had gradually built my new life in Zeeland. Fritz Neumann stood less than a hundred meters away, separated from me by floodwater rather than time and circumstance.

I should have been shocked, but what I felt instead was a strange inevitability—as if some part of me had always known we would meet again, had been waiting for this moment since we parted in that Rotterdam attic as the German forces retreated.

Before I could decide what to do—whether to call out, to wade through the water toward him, to retreat into the church and avoid this unexpected collision of past and present—Fritz turned fully in my direction. His gaze, scanning the area for anyone else needing evacuation, found me standing motionless on the church steps.

Even across the distance and through the still-falling rain, I saw the recognition hit him. His body stiffened, his hands stilling on the rope he had been securing. For a long moment, neither of us moved. Two figures frozen in tableau against the backdrop of ongoing rescue efforts, connected by a shared history no one around us could have guessed.

Then Fritz raised his hand—a small, tentative gesture that might have been greeting or acknowledgment or simply disbelief. I found myself returning it, my arm lifting as if controlled by something other than conscious thought.

The moment broke when a shout came from another rescue boat, calling Fritz's attention to some urgent need. He turned away, responding to the crisis at hand with the same efficiency I remembered from years before. I too was drawn back into the evacuation efforts as another boat arrived at the church steps, needing guidance and assistance.

For the next several hours, I existed in a strange dual reality—physically present in the flood response, helping coordinate resources and people, yet mentally circling the fact of Fritz's presence like a moth around flame. I caught glimpses of him occasionally as he moved through the village with the rescue teams. Once, our eyes met briefly across a cluster of evacuees being guided toward transport. Neither of us acknowledged the other directly, both caught in the more pressing demands of the emergency unfolding around us.

As evening approached, the storm finally began to subside. The rain lessened to a steady drizzle, and the wind, while still strong, no longer threatened to tear roofs from buildings. The water level remained alarmingly high, but at least it had stopped rising. The most vulnerable villagers had been evacuated, leaving primarily the able-bodied who had stayed to assist with rescue efforts or to protect what little remained of their property.

I stood at the church entrance, consulting with Pastor Vos about sleeping arrangements for those who would remain overnight, when a voice behind me—a voice I would have recognised anywhere, anytime—spoke my name.

"Arthijs."

I turned slowly, as if sudden movement might dispel what surely must be an apparition.

But Fritz remained solidly present—older than the man I remembered, lines etched more deeply around his eyes and mouth, his fair hair now threaded with silver at the temples. He wore the practical clothing of the rescue workers—waterproof coat, heavy boots, a woollen cap clutched in one hand—but carried himself with the same controlled precision I remembered from Rotterdam.

"Fritz," I said, my voice sounding strange to my own ears.

Pastor Vos glanced between us, clearly sensing some significance to this meeting but tactful enough not to inquire. "Perhaps you two need a moment," he said, moving away to address another cluster of volunteers.

We stood in awkward silence, eight years and unimaginable changes hanging in the space between us. Up close, I could see the evidence of passing time on Fritz's face—not just the lines and the grey hair, but a weathering, a softening of the sharp edges that had defined his younger self. He had been handsome in a severe way during the war; now his features had relaxed into something gentler, more human.

"You're alive," he said finally, the words carrying more weight than their simplicity suggested.

"So are you." It was an inadequate response, but what could possibly be adequate in such a moment?

Another silence, broken only by the background noises of the ongoing crisis—voices calling instructions, the lapping of water against stone, the distant sound of rescue vehicles on higher ground.

"You're with the rescue teams?" I asked, seeking refuge in practical matters.

Fritz nodded. "I was in Antwerp when news of the flood reached us. I volunteered immediately." A brief hesitation. "I've been living in Belgium since '47."

I absorbed this information—the proximity we had unknowingly maintained, separated by a border but not the vast distance I had imagined when I allowed myself to wonder about his fate.

"And you're here," he continued, his gaze taking in my sodden clothes, my position at the church entrance. "You live in the village?"

"Since '45. After Rotterdam." I gestured vaguely toward the flooded streets. "My house is there. Or was."

Something passed across Fritz's features—a shadow of emotion quickly controlled. "I'm sorry," he said quietly. "To lose another home."

The simple acknowledgment of my past losses—the Rotterdam bakery, the life I had built before hiding—opened something in me that I had kept carefully sealed for years. Not grief exactly, but a recognition so profound it bordered on physical pain.

He remembered. He knew me.

Before I could respond, a call came from outside—another rescue boat arriving with evacuees needing shelter. The moment fractured as we both turned toward the immediate need, professional instincts overriding personal concerns.

"I have to..." I began.

"Of course." Fritz nodded. "Later, perhaps. When things are calmer."

I returned his nod and moved to help the new arrivals, aware of him watching me briefly before he turned to rejoin his team. The interaction had lasted perhaps two minutes, yet it had shifted something fundamental in the careful architecture of my reconstructed life.

Fritz was here. Fritz was alive. Fritz remembered.

The night that followed was long and difficult. More evacuees arrived as outlying areas were reached by rescue teams. Resources stretched thin. The church, while safe from flooding, grew crowded and uncomfortable. Sleep came in brief intervals between urgent tasks and quieter moments of reflection that I couldn't seem to avoid.

I saw Fritz occasionally as he came and went with various rescue groups, but our interactions remained limited to nods of acknowledgment or brief exchanges about immediate needs. The crisis demanded our attention, leaving no space for the conversation we both seemed to recognise was inevitable.

Dawn broke on a transformed landscape. The floodwaters still stood waist-high in much of the village, but the storm had passed completely, leaving an eerie stillness in its wake.

The sky cleared to reveal the full extent of the disaster—buildings damaged or destroyed, debris scattered across the newly formed waterscape, the broken dike visible in the distance as a jagged wound in what should have been our protection.

As morning advanced, official rescue and relief operations became more organised. Military units arrived with boats and equipment. Medical teams established a treatment area in the church. Food and water arrived from unaffected regions. The impromptu community that had formed during the crisis began to transition toward more formal structures and procedures.

I found myself assigned to help distribute supplies, my experience at the bakery making me a natural choice for food management. The work was demanding but straightforward—inventorying donations, organizing distribution, ensuring that rationing was fair and adequate. It occupied my hands and much of my mind, though not enough to completely suppress awareness of Fritz's continued presence in the village.

Late in the afternoon, as the distribution effort paused during a shift change among the rescue teams, I stepped outside the church for a moment of solitude. The air was clear and cold, the winter sun casting long shadows across the still-flooded village. From this elevated position, I could see both the devastation and the first signs of recovery—boats moving purposefully rather than frantically, people salvaging possessions from accessible buildings, the beginning of assessment and planning rather than mere reaction.

"May I join you?"

Fritz's voice came from behind me, quiet but distinct. I turned to find him standing a few meters away, his expression carefully neutral but his eyes betraying an uncertainty I had rarely seen during our years in the attic.

I nodded, and he moved to stand beside me at the low wall surrounding the church grounds. For several minutes, we simply observed the activity below in silence—not the uncomfortable silence of our earlier encounter, but something closer to the companionable quiet we had sometimes shared in Rotterdam when circumstances allowed.

"They're saying it's the worst flood in centuries," Fritz said eventually. "Hundreds dead across the delta. Thousands of homes destroyed."

"It will take years to rebuild," I agreed. "Some areas may never recover fully."

Another silence, this one weighted with approaching personal territory.

"I looked for you," Fritz said finally, his gaze still directed outward across the flooded landscape. "After the war. I went back to Rotterdam in '47, when travel became possible again. The house was occupied by others. No one knew what had happened to you."

The revelation stirred something complicated within me—surprise that he had sought me out, regret for the missed connection, curiosity about what might have been different had he found me then.

"I couldn't stay in Rotterdam," I said. "Too many ghosts."

Fritz nodded, understanding without needing elaboration. "I couldn't return to Germany. Not after..." He trailed off, then continued more firmly. "Belgium was close enough to feel familiar but far enough to be a new beginning."

"What have you been doing there?" I asked, genuinely curious about the life he had built after the uniform was gone.

A small smile touched his lips. "Teaching. Languages and mathematics at a small school in Antwerp." He glanced at me. "Not quite the engineering career I once planned, but satisfying in its way."

I could picture it—Fritz in a classroom, precise and thorough, challenging his students to think clearly. It suited him more than the uniform ever had.

"And you?" he asked. "The bakery?"

"Yes. Not my own, but a good position. I'm head baker now." I gestured toward the submerged village. "Or was, until yesterday."

"You'll rebuild," Fritz said with quiet certainty. "This village, your life here. The Dutch have always rebuilt after the water comes."

His confidence should have seemed presumptuous coming from a German who had spent only a day in our devastated community. Yet it felt instead like a continuation of something he had offered during our years in hiding—a steady belief in survival and continuation when circumstances suggested otherwise.

The sun was beginning to set, casting a golden light across the floodwaters that transformed the disaster zone into something almost beautiful in its otherworldliness. We watched as the light shifted and faded, both perhaps remembering other evenings when we had observed the changing sky through an attic window, grateful for another day of successful hiding.

"I found the photograph," I said abruptly, breaking the extended silence. "After you left. In the house in Rotterdam."

Fritz tensed beside me, understanding immediately what I meant. "Ah," he said softly. "The group photo with the senior officers."

"Yes." I turned to look at him directly. "You never told me your true position. How high you were in the occupation administration."

His pale eyes met mine, unflinching despite the weight of the subject. "Would it have mattered? Would you have trusted me less if you had known?"

The questions were not defensive but genuinely inquiring, as if he himself had wondered the same things during our years of separation.

"I don't know," I admitted. "It was easier to believe you were a reluctant conscript, a minor official caught in something you didn't believe in. The photograph suggested something... more deliberate."

Fritz was quiet for a moment, considering. "I was assigned to the Rotterdam administration because of my language abilities and organisational skills," he said finally. "I was promoted quickly for the same reasons. By 1943, I was senior enough to attend meetings with the regional commanders." His mouth tightened. "But I never volunteered for any of it, Arthijs. I was drafted in '39, before the invasion of Poland. Before I understood what we would become."

I studied his face, looking for the truth behind the words. This was the conversation we had never fully had in the attic—the extent of his complicity, the nature of his service to a regime that had sought to destroy people like me.

"When did you understand?" I asked. "When did you know what Germany was doing to Jews, to others it considered undesirable?"

Fritz's gaze dropped briefly, then returned to mine with a directness that seemed like its own form of atonement. "Earlier than I admitted to myself," he said quietly. "The signs were there by '41, if one was willing to see them. The mass deportations. The properties seized. The people who disappeared and never returned." He shook his head slightly. "I told myself they were being relocated. That conditions in the camps were harsh but not... not what they actually were. I chose ignorance because the alternative was unbearable."

His honesty disarmed me. I had spent years trying to reconcile the Fritz who had saved me with the Fritz who had served the Reich. Had created elaborate explanations and justifications to resolve the contradiction. Yet here he was, offering neither excuses nor self-flagellation, but simply the complicated truth of human compromise and selective blindness.

"Yet you risked everything to hide me," I said, returning to the fundamental paradox of our shared history.

"Yes." Fritz met my gaze steadily. "Because when I saw you by the river that first day, you became real in a way the abstractions never could be. Not just a Jew, but a person. Someone with a name, a history, a future that deserved to exist." He hesitated. "And someone who was like me in ways that mattered."

The reference to our shared secret—the aspects of ourselves that both Nazi Germany and postwar society condemned—hung between us, acknowledged but not directly named even now, years after the immediate danger had passed.

"I never thanked you properly," I said, the words inadequate but necessary. "For the risk you took. For my life."

Fritz shook his head. "You don't owe me gratitude, Arthijs. What I did—it was the bare minimum of human decency in a time when that had become exceptional." A shadow crossed his features. "And it came too late for too many others."

The sun had set completely now, darkness settling over the flooded village. Lights appeared in the church behind us as lamps were lit for the evening. The rescue boats had returned to shore, their work suspended until morning. In the distance, the broken dike stood as a dark line against the night sky, a reminder of how quickly security could be breached, how suddenly the waters could rise.

"What happens now?" I asked, the question encompassing more than the immediate crisis.

Fritz seemed to understand its broader implications. "The relief effort will continue. Reconstruction will begin. Life will gradually return to something resembling normal." He glanced at me. "But you were asking about us, weren't you?"

The directness startled me, though it shouldn't have. Fritz had always been precise in his use of language, careful but not evasive once he decided to speak.

"Yes," I admitted. "I was."

He turned to face me fully, his expression serious but not closed. "I don't know, Arthijs. I don't know if there can be an 'us' in any sense after everything that happened. Too much history between us. Too many complications." He paused. "But I am glad to have found you again. To know that you survived. That you built a life."

The honesty was both painful and refreshing—an acknowledgment of the obstacles without dismissing the possibility that they might be surmountable. It was more than I had expected, perhaps more than I deserved given my own ambivalence about what Fritz had represented in my life.

"I'm glad too," I said simply. "To see you again. To know you continued."

A call came from the church doorway—someone seeking Fritz for consultation about the next day's rescue operations. The moment of privacy was ending, reality reasserting its demands.

"I have to go," Fritz said, echoing our exchange from earlier in the day. "But perhaps, when things are calmer..." He let the suggestion hang, unfinished but clear.

"Yes," I replied. "When things are calmer."

He nodded once, a gesture containing acknowledgment, promise, and a measure of farewell. Then he turned and walked back toward the church, his figure silhouetted against the lamplight spilling from its open doors.

I remained by the wall a few minutes longer, watching the darkness settle more completely over the transformed landscape of Zeeland. The flood had come without warning, had destroyed what we had built, had forced evacuation and adaptation and a complete reconsideration of what security meant. Yet even in this devastation, something unexpected had emerged—a connection I had thought permanently severed, a possibility I had not allowed myself to consider.

Fritz was alive. Fritz was here. And whatever complications our shared history presented, whatever obstacles stood between us, the simple fact of his presence felt like its own kind of watershed—a dividing line between before and after, between acceptance of solitude and the possibility of connection.

The flood waters would recede eventually. The village would rebuild, as Dutch communities had rebuilt after water-related disasters for centuries. My own life would resume its course, altered but continuing.

But something had shifted fundamentally, like the land beneath a broken dike. The careful walls I had constructed around memory and possibility had been breached, allowing what I had kept contained to flow outward into the present.

I turned finally and walked back toward the church, toward warmth and light and the communal response to crisis that had always been humanity's greatest strength. Toward Fritz and whatever conversation might follow when the immediate emergency had passed.

The sea had taken much from us that night.

But it had also given something back.

A second chance.

CHAPTER 18: SECOND CHANCES

Zeeland, 1953-1954

The waters receded slowly from Zeeland, revealing a landscape forever altered. The flood had not only reshaped the physical terrain but had transformed something fundamental within me as well. As buildings emerged from the murky depths, damaged but standing, I found myself similarly surfacing—changed, scarred, but somehow more whole than I had been before.

Fritz remained in the village long after the initial emergency had passed. What began as part of the rescue operation evolved into involvement with reconstruction efforts. His fluency in both Dutch and German proved valuable in coordinating with international aid teams, and his methodical approach to organisation helped bring order to the chaos of rebuilding. When questioned about his extended stay, he spoke of professional obligation and humanitarian duty. But we both knew the truth beneath these practical explanations.

We were circling each other cautiously, neither quite ready to name what was happening between us.

Our conversations in those early weeks were careful, conducted in the public spaces of a community focused on survival and recovery. We spoke of immediate needs—construction materials, food distribution, temporary housing. The weight of our shared history remained present but unaddressed, as if by mutual agreement we had decided to build something new before excavating the past.

On a surprisingly warm evening in late March, nearly two months after the flood, Fritz found me working alone on the reconstruction of the bakery. Visser had decided to rebuild despite his age, claiming that retirement would "finish him faster than any flood could." I had been helping with the repairs each evening after spending my days on the reconstruction of my own small house.

"You still have flour on your face," Fritz observed, standing in the doorway of the half-rebuilt shop. "Some things never change."

I looked up from the shelving I was installing, surprised by both his presence and the gentle teasing in his tone. It was the first time either of us had directly referenced our shared past, however obliquely.

"Hazard of the profession," I replied, brushing at my cheek and probably making it worse. "Though these days it's more likely to be sawdust than flour."

Fritz smiled, a real smile that reached his eyes, and I was struck by how rarely I had seen that expression during our years in Rotterdam. The weight of occupation and deception had pressed down on us both then, making such simple human moments nearly impossible.

He stepped into the bakery, glancing around at the progress we had made. "Visser says you'll be reopening within the month."

"If the supply chains improve, yes." I set down my tools, suddenly aware that we were alone for the first time since the night of the flood. "The ovens are functional again. That's the most important part."

Fritz nodded, running his hand along a newly installed countertop. "You love this work, don't you? The baking."

"I do," I admitted. "It makes sense to me in a way few things do. The precision of it. The transformation of simple ingredients into something... nourishing." I paused, then added quietly, "Noah taught me that. At the Rotterdam bakery."

Fritz's expression softened at the mention of Noah, though we had never discussed my former mentor during the hiding years. "He was the owner? The one who died in the bombing?"

"Yes." I felt a familiar pang at the memory. "He was more than an employer. He was..." I hesitated, searching for the right words. "He saw me. The real me. And accepted what he saw."

Fritz was quiet for a moment, his gaze steady on mine. "Like David," he said softly.

The name hung in the air between us. I had mentioned David only once to Fritz, during our years in the attic—a brief reference to losing someone in the bombing. That he remembered, that he understood the significance, was both surprising and deeply moving.

"Yes," I managed. "Like David."

Fritz moved closer, stopping an arm's length away. "I've wanted to ask about him. Many times. But I wasn't sure I had the right."

The question of rights—who had them, who deserved them, who could claim them—had shaped both our lives in profound ways. Who had the right to live freely? Who had the right to love? Who had the right to ask for forgiveness, to offer understanding, to seek connection?

"You can ask," I said, the words feeling monumental despite their simplicity. "About anything."

And so we talked—truly talked—for the first time since our reunion. As dusk fell over the half-rebuilt bakery, Fritz helped me finish the shelving, our hands working while our voices tentatively built bridges across the years of separation.

I told him about David—his warmth, his humour, his courage in fleeing Germany when so many couldn't or wouldn't recognise the danger. Fritz shared stories of his life in Belgium after the war, of the small school where he taught, of the careful anonymity he had cultivated in a place where his German accent still prompted sidelong glances and sudden silences.

We spoke of the intervening years, of how the world had changed and how we had changed with it. Of the Cold War tensions that had replaced the hot conflict of our youth. Of the slow, incomplete reckoning with what had happened during those dark years—the trials, the denials, the uncomfortable compromises of collective memory.

What we didn't speak of, at least not directly, was what might come next. The fragile possibility taking shape between us remained unnamed, too tentative yet for definition or declaration.

As we said goodnight outside the bakery, Fritz hesitated, then asked, "May I see you tomorrow? Perhaps away from the reconstruction. There's a café on the high ground that's reopened."

The invitation was both ordinary and extraordinary—a simple suggestion between two people, yet laden with the complication of everything we had been to each other and might become.

"Yes," I said, surprising myself with the lack of hesitation. "I'd like that."

The village noticed, of course. In such a small community, little escaped observation and discussion. At first, the attention was muted, overshadowed by the more pressing concerns of flood recovery. But as spring advanced and reconstruction progressed, our increasingly frequent meetings became subject to speculation.

"The German is still here," I overheard Mevrouw de Wit telling her friend at the temporary market set up in the church hall. "Always with van Leeuwen from the bakery. Every evening at Café Zeezicht."

"They were together during the war somehow," her companion replied with the confidence of the utterly uninformed. "Resistance work, my nephew thinks. The German was a spy for the Allies."

The irony might have been amusing if it weren't so painful. The truth—that Fritz had been not a spy but a Wehrmacht officer, that our connection had formed not through resistance heroics but in an attic hiding place—was beyond their imagination and understanding.

Hannah Bakker, who knew more of my history than most, approached the subject with characteristic directness one afternoon as we both volunteered at the distribution centre.

"Your German friend," she said, handing me a box of supplies to be inventoried. "He's staying, isn't he? Not just for the reconstruction."

I met her gaze, finding only genuine interest rather than judgment. "I think so. Though we haven't discussed it specifically."

Hannah nodded, contemplating this. "It will be difficult," she said finally. "Not just the usual prejudices about two men, though those are real enough. But a German, here... only eight years after liberation. Many haven't forgotten. Or forgiven."

"I know." I continued unpacking the box, focusing on the task to steady myself. "But if anyone should have the right to make that decision, shouldn't it be someone who lost everything to the occupation? Who knows exactly what forgiveness costs?"

Hannah's eyes widened slightly, realization dawning. "He was part of it," she said quietly. "The occupation forces."

I nodded, the admission both terrifying and liberating. "And yet he saved me. Hid me for years at tremendous risk to himself." I met her gaze directly. "Life is rarely as simple as we wish it to be, Hannah. People are rarely all one thing or another."

She was silent for a long moment, absorbing this. Then, unexpectedly, she smiled. "My mother used to say that God sends us our greatest challenges and our greatest healings in the same package. We just have to be wise enough to recognise both." She squeezed my arm gently. "Be happy, Arthijs. If anyone has earned that right, it's you."

But not everyone in the village shared Hannah's perspective. As spring turned to summer and Fritz's continued presence became a fixture rather than an emergency measure, the whispers grew louder, the glances more pointed.

Pastor Vos, who had worked closely with Fritz during the flood response, maintained a public stance of respect toward him. But even he approached me one Sunday after services, his expression troubled.

"There are concerns, Arthijs," he said, choosing his words carefully. "About your... friendship with the German."

"His name is Fritz," I replied, more sharply than I had intended. "Fritz Neumann."

The pastor nodded, accepting the correction. "With Fritz, then. You must understand that for many here, especially the older residents, the wounds of occupation are still fresh. Five years of hunger, fear, oppression... these are not easily forgotten."

"No," I agreed. "They aren't. Nor should they be."

"Yet you have clearly found a way to move beyond that history with him." Pastor Vos studied me with genuine curiosity. "May I ask how? What allows you to separate the man from what his country did to ours?"

It was the most direct question anyone had posed about my relationship with Fritz, and it deserved an honest answer. But how could I explain the complex reality without revealing too much? Without exposing secrets that still carried risk in a world not ready to understand?

"I judge him by his actions," I said finally. "By what he did when faced with impossible choices. By who he proved to be when testing came." I met the pastor's gaze steadily. "And I remember that Christ himself told us to love our enemies—perhaps the most difficult commandment of all, but also the most transformative when actually practiced."

Pastor Vos's eyebrows rose slightly at having his own theological principles turned so neatly toward defence of a former occupier. A thoughtful smile touched his lips. "Touché, Arthijs. Though I suspect there's more to your history with Fritz than you're sharing."

"There is," I acknowledged. "But it's a story for another time, perhaps."

The pastor nodded, accepting this boundary. "Know that you are both welcome here," he said, gesturing toward the church. "Whatever others may say or think. This remains a house of reconciliation for all who seek it."

His support, while conditional and perhaps not fully informed, provided a measure of protection as summer progressed and Fritz's position in the village solidified. When the school announced plans to reopen in September with additional language instruction to prepare students for an increasingly international world, Fritz was offered a teaching position. The practical need for his skills provided official sanction for his continued presence, though it didn't eliminate the underlying tensions.

Those tensions came to a head in early August, during a community meeting to discuss the ongoing reconstruction efforts. The meeting had been proceeding routinely until Hendrick Klaassen, who had lost his fishing boat and nearly his life in the flood, stood to address a question about the rebuilding schedule.

"Why is a German making these decisions for us?" he demanded, pointing at Fritz who had been reviewing the construction timeline. "Haven't we had enough of Germans telling us what to do, when to do it, how to live our lives?"

A uncomfortable silence fell over the village hall. Fritz remained standing at the front, his expression carefully neutral though I could see the tension in his shoulders, the slight whitening of his knuckles as he gripped the edge of the table.

"Meneer Neumann is part of the international aid coordination," Mayor van Dam replied, his tone deliberately measured. "His expertise has been invaluable in securing resources for our community."

"And before that?" Klaassen pressed. "Where was he during the war? What was he doing while our people were starving, while our young men were being taken for labour camps?"

The questions hung in the air, dangerous and electric. I found myself half-rising from my seat, though I had no clear plan of what to say or do.

Before I could act, an unexpected voice broke the silence.

"He was helping people survive."

Every head turned toward Hannah Bakker, who stood calmly near the back of the hall.

"None of us came through the war with completely clean hands," she continued. "We all made compromises to survive. We all looked away sometimes when looking directly would have required action we weren't brave enough to take." Her gaze swept the room, settling briefly on various faces. "And some of us—a very few—found the courage to act despite the risk. To help others even when it endangered themselves."

Her eyes found Fritz, then me. "I don't know exactly what Meneer Neumann did during the war. But I know what he's doing now—helping rebuild what nature destroyed, just as we're all trying to rebuild what war destroyed. Perhaps that's the most any of us can do after such loss. Begin again. Try to be better this time."

The tension in the room shifted, not dissipating entirely but changing quality. Hannah's words had named something many felt but few had articulated—the complex reality of survival and its aftermath, the universality of compromise, the possibility of redemption through action rather than words.

Klaassen sat down, not entirely satisfied but momentarily silenced. The meeting continued, the immediate crisis averted though the underlying issues remained. As people filed out afterward, I found Hannah waiting near the door.

"Thank you," I said simply.

She smiled, a hint of mischief in her eyes. "I meant every word. But I also said it for completely selfish reasons." At my questioning look, she continued, "If this village can accept a German teacher who may have been part of the occupation, perhaps someday it can accept a woman schoolteacher who lives with another woman schoolteacher as more than just 'roommates.'"

I stared at her, understanding dawning. "You and Mevrouw de Jong...?"

Hannah's smile widened slightly. "We survivors must stick together, Arthijs. All of us who live with secrets the world isn't ready to hear." She squeezed my arm gently. "Be happy with your Fritz. Build something good from all this destruction."

As she walked away, I felt something shift within me—a recognition that our story, Fritz's and mine, existed within a broader tapestry of human connection persisting despite societal constraints. That what we were tentatively building was not as isolated or impossible as I had feared.

When Fritz emerged from the hall, his face still tight with the tension of the confrontation, I made a decision. I walked directly to him, close enough that anyone watching would see clear intention in the movement.

"Come home with me," I said quietly. "We have things to discuss that can't be said here."

His eyes widened slightly, understanding the multiple meanings in my invitation. "Are you certain?"

I nodded. "It's time to stop hiding, Fritz. In all the ways that matter."

That night, in the small house I had rebuilt after the flood, we finally spoke without reservations or careful boundaries. About Rotterdam and the attic years. About the weight of secrets kept and now potentially shared. About what we had been to each other then and what we might become now, in this imperfect but possible aftermath.

"I never thought I would have this chance," Fritz said as we sat across from each other at my kitchen table, lamplight casting warm shadows around us. "To see you again. To explain. To ask if there might be..." He hesitated, searching for words. "A future of some kind. For us."

The question contained multitudes—practical concerns about how two men might build a life together in a world still hostile to such connections, emotional complexities given our shared history, moral considerations about forgiveness and redemption that had no simple resolution.

"I don't know exactly what form it would take," I replied honestly. "But yes, I think there could be a future." I reached across the table, placing my hand over his. "I want there to be."

The touch—deliberate, intentional, chosen rather than accidental or furtive—bridged more than just the physical distance between us. It connected Rotterdam to Zeeland, past to present, what we had survived to what we might yet build.

Fritz turned his hand beneath mine, our fingers interlacing. "It won't be easy," he said. "The village, the past, the world as it is..."

"No," I agreed. "But what part of our lives has been easy? We've survived worse than disapproving neighbours."

A smile touched his lips, genuine and warm. "We have at that."

As autumn approached and Fritz's teaching position at the village school began, we established patterns that allowed us to build a life together while maintaining the necessary public discretion. Fritz rented a room in a house near the school, but spent most evenings at my place, officially helping with ongoing repairs or sharing meals as "friends" often did in the close-knit post-flood community.

The reality of our relationship remained unspoken yet increasingly understood by those closest to us. Hannah and her partner Johanna occasionally joined us for dinner, the four of us creating a small island of acceptance in a sea of convention. Pastor Vos, with his gentle wisdom, never asked direct questions but offered subtle support through inclusion and respect.

There were difficult moments, of course. Times when someone would make a casual remark about "the German" in my presence, not realizing the pain such distancing language caused. Occasions when Fritz's accent would trigger visible discomfort in older villagers who had suffered directly under occupation. The constant small adaptations and concealments required by a society not ready to acknowledge love that didn't fit prescribed patterns.

But there were beautiful moments too. Quiet evenings by the fire, Fritz reading poetry aloud in his precise German while I baked bread in the small kitchen. Sunday afternoons walking along the rebuilt dikes, watching the sea that had nearly destroyed us now contained again by human determination and engineering. The gradual, remarkable experience of being known fully—history, flaws, and all— and accepted nonetheless.

By the spring of 1954, as Zeeland bloomed with reconstruction and renewal, what had begun as tentative possibility had solidified into something real and lasting. We were building a life together—discrete in public but authentic in private, mindful of social limitations but not defined by them.

"I've been offered a permanent position at the school," Fritz told me one evening as we sat in my garden, watching the sunset paint the sky in shades of orange and rose. "The language program has been successful enough that they want to expand it next year."

"That's wonderful," I said, genuinely pleased for him. Teaching suited Fritz—his precision, his patience, his ability to see potential in those still developing their capabilities.

"It means I'd be staying," he continued, a question in his voice. "Permanently. Here in the village."

I turned to him, understanding the real query beneath his statement. "I want you to stay," I said simply. "Here, with me. For as long as we have."

Fritz's expression softened, relief and joy mingling in his pale eyes. "Even with everything that came before? The uniform, the war, the complications I bring to your life here?"

I considered this, wanting my answer to hold the full truth rather than mere reassurance. "I've learned that life is rarely pure or simple," I said finally. "We're all marked by our histories, all carrying burdens of choice and circumstance. The question isn't whether those marks exist, but what we do with them. How we carry them forward."

I reached for his hand, a gesture that had become natural between us despite the caution we maintained in public. "You saved my life in Rotterdam, Fritz. Now, in a different way, you're helping me live it. That's what matters to me."

He squeezed my hand, emotion making speech difficult for a moment. When he did speak, his voice was low but certain. "I love you, Arthijs. I think perhaps I have since those days in the attic, though I wouldn't have called it that then. Couldn't have."

The words, never spoken directly during our years together, hung in the evening air between us—a declaration both ordinary and extraordinary, like so much about our shared story.

"And I love you," I replied, the truth of it settling into me with the weight of recognition rather than revelation. This wasn't new feeling but newly acknowledged, the naming of something that had been growing quietly through all the years of separation and reconnection.

As darkness fell around us, the first stars appearing in the clear spring sky, I thought about the strange paths that had brought us to this moment. The Rotterdam bombing that had taken David from me. The years of hiding that had connected Fritz and me in ways neither of us could have anticipated. The flood that had reunited us when all hope of connection seemed lost.

Second chances rarely came wrapped as expected. They emerged from disaster, from loss, from the ruins of what had been planned or hoped for. They required courage to recognise and more courage still to grasp. But in their imperfect, complicated reality lay possibilities for healing that perfect, unblemished lives might never encounter.

Fritz and I had been granted such a chance—not despite our complicated past but somehow because of it. We had been transformed by what we had survived, shaped by the choices made in our darkest moments, connected by recognitions that transcended the divisions others created and maintained.

Now, in this small Zeeland village rebuilding itself after disaster, we were creating something new from the fragments of our past lives. Not perfect, not unmarked by history's scars, but real and sustaining nonetheless.

A second chance, hard-won but precious beyond measure.

EPILOGUE

Zeeland, 1975

The sea was calm today.

I stood by the dunes, feeling the cold wind lift the edges of my coat. The waves rolled in quietly, their rhythm steady, unchanging. After all these years, I still found myself drawn to this spot—the place where the flood had nearly taken everything, and where, in the end, it had given me back the only thing that had ever truly mattered.

I reached into my pocket and pulled out a cigarette. My hands trembled as I lit it, though whether from age or memory, I wasn't sure anymore. The doctor had told me to stop smoking, but after everything my body had endured, what harm could one more cigarette do?

Footsteps crunched in the sand behind me.

"You're going to stand out here and freeze?"

I smiled, not turning. "I like the cold."

Fritz stepped up beside me, his hands tucked deep into his coat pockets. His blond hair had faded to silver, his face lined with the weight of the years. But his eyes—those same blue eyes that had found me in the dark all those years ago—still held the same sharpness, the same quiet strength.

"You're thinking too much," he murmured.

I exhaled smoke, watching it disappear into the sea air. "Maybe."

He studied me for a long moment, then sighed. "Come inside."

"In a minute."

He hesitated, then reached out, his fingers brushing against mine. Even after all these years, we were careful. Always careful. Even here, in the quiet of Zeeland, where people had learned to tolerate us with the same silent disapproval they reserved for harsh winters and high tides.

They had never truly accepted us.

A Dutchman and a German. A Jew and a former soldier. Two men living together as more than just friends.

We had learned to live in the spaces between. The glances exchanged behind closed doors. The quiet moments in the safety of our home. The knowledge that, to the world outside, we would always be something to be whispered about.

It had not been easy.

When we first settled here after the war, people had spat at Fritz's feet when he walked through the market. He never reacted, never spoke a word in German unless we were alone. He had learned Dutch quickly, out of necessity, though his accent never quite faded.

For me, it had been different. I had returned to a world that barely existed anymore. My family was gone. The bakery in Rotterdam was gone. Everything I had known before the war had been reduced to ashes. I was a survivor, but in some ways, I was a ghost.

And ghosts had no place in the world of the living.

We had kept our heads down. Worked hard. Built a life out of the pieces left behind. Fritz had continued teaching at the village school until his retirement last year, his students now grown with children of their own. I had eventually opened my own small bakery, though my hands were slower now, my body not as strong as it once was.

For twenty-two years, we had endured.

Through slurs muttered under breath. Through landlords who refused to rent to us. Through old war wounds that never fully healed—not just the ones on our bodies, but the ones in our minds.

And yet, through it all, we had stayed together.

Because even on the worst days, when I could not bear to see my reflection in the mirror, when Fritz's hands shook from nightmares of orders he had once obeyed, when we both sat in silence, burdened by the weight of the past—we had each other.

I had never believed in fate. But I had believed in Fritz.

And he had never left me behind.

I took a final drag from my cigarette, then flicked it into the sand.

"Alright," I said, turning to him. "Let's go home."

He nodded and fell into step beside me as we walked back toward the house. It was small, weathered by the salt air, but it was ours.

Inside, the fire crackled in the hearth. The scent of coffee lingered in the air. The walls were lined with books—some in Dutch, some in German, some in English, collected over the years like artifacts from another life.

Fritz lowered himself into the chair by the fire with a quiet groan.

"We're getting old," he muttered.

I chuckled. "You are."

He shot me a look, but there was warmth in it. A softness that only ever existed in these quiet moments, when the world outside couldn't see us.

I sat across from him, pouring two cups of coffee. I handed him one, our fingers brushing.

We didn't speak. We didn't need to.

Outside, the wind howled over the dunes, but in here, there was warmth. In here, there was home.

Fritz lifted his cup slightly. "To us."

I raised mine in return. "To us."

This morning, a letter had arrived from America. From a young woman writing a book about survivors' stories. She had found my name in an old registry, had tracked me through records of the bakery. She wanted to interview me, to hear my experience during the occupation.

"For the younger generation," she had written. "So they understand. So they remember."

I hadn't decided yet if I would agree. There was so much I still couldn't speak about—the cupboard's suffocating darkness, the attic's silent terror, the constant fear that hummed beneath every moment of those years.

And there was Fritz. How could I tell our story without revealing him? Without exposing the German officer who had saved a Jewish man, who had risked everything for a secret neither of us could fully acknowledge even now, decades later?

"You should do it," Fritz said, as if reading my thoughts. "Tell her."

I looked at him, surprised. "Everything?"

His eyes met mine, steady and clear. "Everything. It's time, Arthijs."

He was right, as he often was about such things. Our story wasn't just ours anymore. It belonged to history—to the complex, messy truth of how people behaved during humanity's darkest hours. Some with cruelty. Some with indifference. And some, like Fritz, with unexpected courage.

The world was changing. Slowly, perhaps, but changing nonetheless. What had seemed impossible in 1945 or even 1955—speaking openly of my Jewish identity, of my years in hiding, of my life with Fritz—now felt, if not easy, then at least possible.

"What would I even say?" I asked. "Where would I begin?"

Fritz smiled, the lines around his eyes deepening. "Begin with the truth. That in the darkest times, humanity reveals itself—both the terrible and the beautiful."

"And which were we?" I asked, the question that had haunted us both for decades.

"We were human," he said simply. "Flawed. Frightened. Doing what we could with what we had." He reached across the small table between us, taking my hand in his—a gesture that had become as natural as breathing. "And we found each other. Against everything that should have kept us apart."

I nodded, feeling the familiar ache of memory alongside the warmth of present connection.

Perhaps that was the message worth sharing. Not just the horror of what had happened—the bombs, the hunger, the hiding, the constant fear—but also this. The possibility of finding connection even in the midst of destruction. The resilience of the human spirit that allowed not just for survival but for love.

"I'll write to her tomorrow," I decided. "Tell her I'll do the interview."

Fritz squeezed my hand, his eyes bright with emotion. "Good."

Outside, the day was fading, the early winter darkness settling over Zeeland. Another day passing, another added to the thousands we had somehow been granted together.

We were the lucky ones. We had survived when so many hadn't. We had found each other when all hope seemed lost. We had built a life from the ruins of war, a connection that transcended the boundaries others drew between us.

It hadn't been perfect. It hadn't been easy. The nightmares still came. The memories still haunted. The world still didn't fully have a place for people like us.

But we had peace. We had each other. We had survived.

And for now, for this moment by the fire as the wind sang outside our windows, that was everything.

Printed in Great Britain
by Amazon